Spearmint Leaves

Spearmint Leaves

Ben Pleasants

About the Author

Ben Pleasants is a noted playwright. His plays include *The Gluttons* (1970), *Winter in Mongolia* (1975), *The Hemingway/Dos Passos Wars* (1998), *Contentious Minds: The Mary McCarthy/Lillian Hellman Affair* (2002), and the upcoming *The Ghosts of Pumpkin Park* (2011).

His next novel is *The Victory of Defeat*.

ONE

They were not twins; they were not even sisters. They were first cousins and as little girls no one could tell them apart. Born in Greenwich Connecticut on the same day, April 12, 1975, they had not seen each other since they were eight years old.

The O'Brien Brothers, Tom and Bill, owners of an advertising agency in New York City, lived next door to each other in matching Tudor mansions, and Ariel and Miranda spent every day of their first eight years together. In the same classes from kindergarten through second grade, their teachers referred to them simply as *the twins*; they could not tell them apart.

In 1983 Miranda's father, Uncle Bill, died of bone cancer, and Miranda's mother moved away.

For a year Ariel spoke of nothing else. "Where is Miranda? Did she die like Uncle Bill? Could I call her on the phone? Would Miranda write?"

To all this Ariel's parents replied: "She has gone far away and will never come back."

Once, when she was ten, Ariel received a postcard from Alaska that read "I miss you so, Miranda," but Ariel's mother tore it up before Ariel could read it. All Ariel could make out from the pieces was the name of a place, Kodiak Island, and Miranda's printed scrawl, which was almost identical to her own.

Then there was nothing, not a sound.

From time to time, as Ariel O'Brien grew to womanhood, traces of their Friendship would come swimming back into her day dreams: a bad case of sunburn on Mystic Beach when they were five; discovering two arrowheads in a farmer's field the next spring; and always the Easter Sunday they had run through a field of daisies in their hats and coats, and ruined their slips when they took off their blouses to compare nipples. Tom O'Brien had always pointed it out. "They are identical down to their purple nipples."

By the age of twenty, Ariel had only a faded Polaroid shot of her cousin Miranda, but as she moved on successfully into a career in modeling, then acting, the memory of her cousin persisted. Once she thought she saw her at a dance in her freshman year at Yale University. And then in New York, when she modeled for a famous fashion photographer, she was shown a photo from a rival agency and was asked "Did you work for Hortense?"

Ariel looked at the photo. "Never."

"She's identical; at least in black and white."

As all thoughts of Miranda began to fade, Ariel O'Brien became a star. Her face was on the cover of every fashion magazine in the country. She was Miss Teen Queen of New England. When she was cast in the starring role in the nighttime teen soap opera, *South Coast High*, she had arrived. Ariel O'Brien.

In 1997 her webpage took forty thousand hits a week. If Miranda had wanted to find her, it would have been easy. Her name and face were everywhere.

Then one evening, taking drugs with her co-star Joshua Perrin, who watched non-stop porno night and day, as he prematurely ejaculated-- not unusual for him--Josh jumped up yelling from the bed, "Air, look at that one, the blonde. Gajezus. I mean, except for the hair and the way they painted her lips, that could be you! I-DEN-tical."

"What?" Ariel was working toward an orgasm as he sprayed her leg with jism.

"Look. That's you. Same boobs, same very black pussy hair, same lips, same ears, even the same asshole." He turned her over to get a better look. "When in hell did you do porno?"

Ariel sat up and came to attention as her orgasm faded. "I *never* did porno."

"Come on. That's you."

"It's just a girl who looks like me. She's blond."

"Not her pussy. If that's not you, Ariel, you must have an identical twin."

"I don't even have a sister."

"Air, her nipples are purple. I been with a lot of girls and none of them ever had nipples that color."

"Josh, it's not me."

"You're blushing. So you made a few fuck films."

"It's not me. I know who it is. Let me borrow the DVD. Okay?"

"You can have it. Sorry I shot off so fast. It's the fucking Ecstasy. I'll get you again in the morning."

"No. I gotta go home."

"You're upset. So you did porno. I did one too. Ten years ago."

Ariel dressed, put on her snakeskin boots, then dropped the DVD into her coat pocket. "It's not me, Josh. It's my cousin. Trust me."

"I do. You never gave me VD."

Ariel slapped him on the cheek and kissed him goodnight.

"See you Saturday?" he asked.

"Yeah."

"You sure that's not you?"

"It's not me. It's my cousin Miranda."

- 2 -

Groves lay behind two yew bushes, focusing his telephoto. Jones was down the hill on his cell phone.

"She just drove off," Groves whispered.

"Did she look mad?"

Groves caught her twice with a 1600 exposure as she rocketed past him in her truck. "Nope, she don't look mad. She looks a little high."

"Here she comes," Jones whispered. "I got her face. It's nothing. Maybe a little wine. Did you get them screwing?"

"I don't know. He was sucking her nipples. You know what they look like. Purple. I'm not sure I got her face. That goddamned long hair was in the way."

"Get some shots of the house?"

"Just the bedroom. They were watching TV." As Groves crawled out from under the yew bush, a lizard slid into his sock. "Shit." He stumbled and rolled backwards down the hill, all the way to the base of Nichol's Canyon.

"For shits sake, Ray, don't break that goddamn lens."

Jones ran down after him with a flashlight, probing a cactus garden. Groves lay on his back, clutching the Hassleblad to his stomach, all bloody with needle sticks.

Jones bent down to rescue the camera. "Nice work. It's in one piece."

"Good. I'm glad the camera's okay. I think I broke my right arm."

Jones snapped the camera and lens back into the metal case, yanking Groves up by his left arm, dumping him gently into the van.

They drove directly to St. John's Hospital. Groves was right. A compound facture of the right humorus. The surgeon sank five steel screws into the bone.

- 3 -

"Mira, for godsake, would you stop the fucking laughter." Hotz, the director, was troubled by the lighting. "Your right leg needs to be two inches higher."

"Do you want him in me or not?"

"Yes, I want him in you." Hotz peered through the camera lens. "What the fuck is *your* problem, Mira? Is it his balls or what?"

Mira was giggling.

Gotthold, who was Swedish, began to laugh too. "Hotz, you know--"

"I didn't ask you for your opinion. You don't have an opinion, God. You only have a prick. Remember that. She's the star."

"Hotz, if I'm the star," said Mira, "then I can tell you what the problem is, okay?"

"Okay. What the fuck is making you laugh? And you, you fucking square head, stop giggling. We got two more angles to shoot, and then the cum shot on her tongue. We're three days behind as it is."

By now Gotthold and Mira were laughing as the cameraman was trying not to snicker.

"Well? Tell me so I can get that wad of cum jiggling around on your pink lips, and we can all go home. Okay?"

"Okay. Hotz, it's the angle. My leg is up so high, every time God puts it in my butt, I fart. That's what it is. And my whole goddamn thigh is cramping up from the camera angle. It's too high. If you insist on a shot with me farting over his cock, okay. But if you want me to feel it, and I really like the way God strokes it up me, then lower the fucking camera and let me feel it as he slides it in. You may not care who jams it up my cunt, but I do. He's not like Slidell with that hairy cock of his that always gets stuck. God's an artist with his rod, and he always comes when you want him too. Right on cue."

The cameraman waved in affirmation.

"Alright, Mira," said Hotz. "You're the star. The star of the moment, anyhow. Lower the goddamn camera, Jake. And what the hell are *you* laughing at?"

"It's just that when she farts, it smells like roses," he said. "That's the porno trade."

They all had a very long laugh. Jake got the shot. Hotz was happy. And Gotthold Roddick came right on cue, all over Mira's pink lips.

Just another day's work in the skin trade.

- 4 -

Ariel O'Brien wasn't stupid. She was a Yale graduate and she had her own production company, Hapless Pictures. It was mostly a tax write-off. Hapless had done no pictures to date. Only one, a comedy about dorm life in a small college, was under consideration. But the write-off did provide Ariel with office space near Universal and a fulltime co-producer, Nancy Ruiz.

Nancy was mostly a secretary, a friend left over from modeling days in New York. She was Ariel's closest friend. They told each other everything. Ariel trusted Nancy with her life, and Nancy had not proved wanting. Nancy read all of Ariel's *South Coast* fan mail, dividing it up into three stacks: friendly, stupid, and life-threatening. One from the last stack, Nancy had turned over to the police in the nick of time.

The fan said he had been to Ariel's beach house and liked the painting on her bedroom wall, a John Piper. Very specific. A rare work. Not your ordinary Miro or Picasso.

The fan's name was Glen Zendorf, and he was halfway up her balcony when the cops arrived. They caught him with a Colt 45, duct tape, an electric vibrator, and a copy of *Catcher in the Rye*.

Nancy was the first line in Ariel's defense against tabloid torturers, always on the lookout for the stalkers from *Flem*: Ray Groves and Bud Jones.

Today, Sunday, Nancy was at the office. She liked to work on Sundays and take off Mondays. Sunday was her catch-up day. Ariel never bothered Nancy on Sunday, but this Sunday was different. Ariel called from her car two blocks from her office.

"Nan, I need a favor. Is this a bad time?"

"No. I'm ordering a new computer. Did you finish the show okay?"

"Yeah. No problems with the redhead this week. Listen, I was at Josh's house last night and he showed me something I need you to check on. Something real private, nobody gets to know about. *Nobody*. Okay?"

"Sure, sure. You know you can trust me. What is it? I'm all ears."

The office door opened and Nancy Ruiz jumped right out of her four inch heels.

"This."

"For Christ sake, Air, that's not funny. Goddamn cell phones!"

Ariel handed her the DVD. "It's porno. Play it. The girl in the fuck film looks just like me, except for the hair."

"Don't get so excited." Nancy popped the DVD into the player. "It'll take a minute."

The title rolled by: *Fashion Sluts*. Starring Mira Monroe and Gotthold Roddick. Ariel and Nancy watched the two actors remove their clothing.

"See," said Ariel. "The name is Mira Monroe. Now look carefully.

The eyes, the mouth, the neck. Even the nipples are the same as mine. Don't you think? Josh says so."

"I've never seen your nipples, except in that layout you did for--"

"Okay, okay. Take my word for it. There. Look at that. We have the same clitoris. She's my cousin, Nan. First cousin. It has to be her. I need to find her fast, before those guy from *Flem* catch up to her. If they find these films and put them on the front page of that rag--"

"Calm down, Ariel. Calm down. It's not you, you told me so."

"Groves and Jones don't know that. They'll be certain I did this film when I was...at Yale."

Nancy laughed. "So you can sue them. By the way, Groves fell down the hill outside your co-star's house last night, and broke his arm in two places. I heard it on the radio."

"He was up at Josh's place? So those were the jerks I passed on my way down the hill. Groves and Jones."

"They're always out there till they get what they need. You want them dead, right?"

Ariel laughed. "You know, Ray Groves is really kind of cute. I wonder if he's fruity?"

"If you truly want him dead, I have a cousin in the business."

"I don't. I don't want anyone dead."

"El Caudillo. He's good, too. He works for the DEA."

"Just look at them, Nan. Gejesus. Call the company. Stupendous Productions. They're in the Valley. The address comes up right before the FBI warning. You know, where they tell you if you copy their film in any way, they'll report you to the government?"

"Air, I watch porno too."

"Write down the address and phone them."

"She sure as hell looks like you, Air. Man."

"I know. The funny thing is, she's a pretty good actress. The way she moves her eyes in the closeups."

Nancy studied Mira Monroe as she was deftly removing her teddy.

"You think she's acting when she's getting it on? Look at that guy. He's so far up her..."

"Gotthold Roddick," Ariel laughed. "That can't be his real name."

"So tell me, who's this cousin of yours?"

"Her real name is Miranda O'Brien. We're first cousins. I knew her when I was little. We were like sisters. Just find her, Nan. Fast, before *Flem* does."

"Okay, okay. I heard you the first time. Chinga! This is my catch-up day. Sunday." She made a few notes. "I'm already working Sundays for you." She smirked.

"Poor you. I'll get you a seat at the Emmys. Next to Josh Perrin."

"How about his seat, with me sitting under him?" Nancy continued watching the DVD. "Man, this is beautiful. They're making porno so pro these days. Even the music is good. Look at her go. Chinga. I mean, the babe's not acting, Air."

"Find her, Nan. Get me a phone number, or an address, or a pager."

"Yeah? Then what? So I find her. What do I say to a porno star who looks like Ariel O'Brien? I mean, really like you, except for the hair?"

Ariel thought for a moment. "Tell her. Hmmmm. Tell Miss Monroe that Stellar Studios saw her latest DVD and they want an audition. Make it interesting. 'Hey, we know you're not a blonde and your real name's Miranda, but a cousin who works with Joshua Perrin would really like to talk to you about a part on *South Coast*. You don't think she'd jump at a legit offer? That chick Traci Lords did."

"Yeah. That might work. I'll try it."

"If I hear from her by Monday, you got a seat under Josh at the Emmys, whether he likes it or not. He'd probably like it."

Nancy smiled. "Good. Now go off flying or something, and let me get my work done. It's Sunday."

- 5 -

Ariel was out was in the yard with the gardener, arranging rocks in her garden, when the call came through.

"Air?"

"Hi, Nan?"

"Guess who I got for you on the other end of the telephone line? On a Sunday, no less?"

"Who?"

"Take a deep breath. Cousin Miranda. Miranda O'Brien, formally of Greenwich, Connecticut. Can you talk?"

"Uh, yes... Let me take a sip of water first. Okay. Put her through."

"Miss Monroe, she's on the line."

There was a brief pause. "Ariel?" Her voice broke.

"My god, Miranda, is that you? After all these years." Ariel chocked back a sob. "Is that really you?" The blood was pounding through her temples.

"It is. Me. How the hell did you find me?"

"Your latest film. *Fashion Sluts*. Josh Perrin, my co-star...he's a fan."

"He's a fan of mine? Oh Jeeeez. Josh Perrin? Ariel..." Her voice broke. "I've wanted to call you for fifteen years. Listen, I'm in makeup, which means they're greasing up my ass with baby oil, but...if we could meet. Face to face. I have so much to tell you." The line clicked twice. "Ariel? You still there?"

"I'm here. I'm still catching my breath."

"Listen, if I could meet you some place in the next day or two. Alone? Some place private. I mean, really private, where there's no one out there with a camera."

"Tell me about it, Miranda. I have a beach house in Malibu. Nan'll give you the address. You'll need a plastic card to get in. Say after nine on Tuesday night?"

"Wonderful. We have a fuck of a lot to talk about, Ariel. You have no idea. It's so great to hear from you. I've been dreading this call for years, but I always hoped I'd see you again somewhere. Just to reach out and grab your sleeve in the mall. Tanya on *South Coast*."

"Oh God, don't remind me. I'm about to do run-throughs with my coach. Talk to Nan. She'll get the card to you and I'll see you at nine on Tuesday night. Okay?"

"Okay."

"Hearing your voice after all these years, Miranda. I'd just given up, but I always loved you like a long lost sister. Do you know what that means?"

"Ariel, you have no idea."

TWO

On Tuesday night Ariel left the studio at 7:45 p.m. It was her fifth year on *South Coast High* and she was bored to death. In the back of her pickup truck were five hundred pounds of crated fieldstone she'd bought for a patio. Ariel liked to do things herself. When Josh and the cast asked her to stick around for a little Democratic fund raiser, she told them the usual: "I don't vote, like half the country, and I've never regretted it."

Anaca, her redheaded nemesis, called her an anarchist.

"I drive like one," she thought, taking the twists and turns on Mulholland Drive at sixty. She could feel the torque of the rocks on the curves as her steel belted radials bit into the mud. It was raining.

Dipping down Beverly Glen onto Sunset, Ariel suddenly recalled her date with Miranda. Mira Monroe. Miranda had been on Ariel's mind all morning, until she launched into the idiocy of this week's script: Anaca, who played her closest friend, and Josh, who was her brother Paul on *South Coast*, were running off to Vegas to elope and it was Tanya's job to locate her parents and break up the elopement before they could reach the chapel. Another episode right out of Chekhov, Ariel thought.

Tuesdays never went right for her. Three days away from *South Coast* were hardly enough to get the poison out of her system.

Ariel needed a year. A whole fucking year away from the great American poison: television. Twice she put in a call to Nancy, but the line was busy. Miranda was scheduled to arrive at her house by nine and Ariel had nothing to serve. No wine, no pastry, no candy, no grass.

She stuck to Sunset avoiding Brentwood. Ariel hated Brentwood.

Brentwood people were always rude to her. In Brentwood, men followed her into the ladies' room and the women stared at her eyes. Brentwood people were always in her face. They argued and cut off people and gave you the finger when you stared them down. No wonder OJ killed his wife in Brentwood. Brentwood people were all potential killers, especially the drivers of BMWs.

Pacific Palisades was better, but it was 8:30 and everything would be closed. She had only one hope, to call her good friend Pat, a Jew who pretended to be Irish. Pat ran a nightclub just up the coast from the Old Getty.

Ariel pulled out her cell phone and speed dialed the number.

"Dublin Club."

"Is Pat there?"

"This is Pat."

"Pat, this is Ariel. O'Brien. I'm desperate."

"It's been a long time, beautiful. Everyone here misses you like hell. And when are you bringing your good friend Josh back?"

"Soon Pat, I promise. Listen, I'm on my way home and I need a few things." The phone clicked and hissed. "Pat? Are you there?"

"Still here. What is it you want, lovely?"

"Well, a good Bordeaux, to start with, and...some pastry. Whatever you got. Fresh flowers. And a few ounces of grass. Is that asking too much?"

"Where are you?"

"About ten minutes away. In my car."

"Well, here's the skinny. Bordeaux's no problem. Henry can handle the grass, from his hands to yours, outside. I'll steal a few flowers from the guy next door. But my pastry's all dried up. How about a lemon cake?"

"Okay. I guess that will have to do. Lemon cake. In that case, throw in a good ZinfAndel."

"I'll put it on your tab. The grass you have to pay for in cash."

"How is my tab?"

"Nancy just paid it. Gotta go, princess. I'm up to my ass in Fenn's for dinner. Don't ask which ones."

"As if I cared. Thanks, Pat. You know I love you." Ariel angled a turn onto PCH and sped up past the Old Getty toward the Dublin Club. Ariel loved the Old Getty, a Roman villa with its ornate gardens and olive trees overlooking the sea, but Rome was closed these days, still in renovation.

She'd gone there for the first time with Josh. A private party. The place had class. People didn't paw her there. The men didn't follow her into the ladies' room.

Five minutes later, in a heavy rain, she pulled up in front of the Dublin Club. It was five before nine. Henry stood outside under an umbrella with flowers and package in hand.

"Here's everything, beautiful. Careful of the flowers. They're Zambidians."

"Nice, Henry. Thanks." She dropped the bag on the floor of her Ford and stuck the flowers on the seat between her purse and her makeup case.

"Here's a hundred, Henry," she said. "It's for the grass."

"Thanks, beautiful. Wanta come in? Pat wants to show you off to all the Fenns."

"I'm late, Henry. Tell him thanks. I'll catch him next time. Promise."

She blew him a kiss with her full wet lips, just catching the curb and shaking the fieldstone in the back of her truck. Rain was coming down hard. It was 9:15 when she slid her card through the check-in gate at Point Dume.

Miranda stood on the top step of Ariel's townhouse, smoking a cheroot.

"Sorry I'm late, cuz," said Ariel.

"Sorry I got here first. Your rocks are all wet." Miranda ran down to meet her.

"I bought us some stuff." Ariel held up the flowers.

They hugged, first gently, then with tightening sobs.

"Could you carry the lemon cake?" Ariel asked.

"I love lemon cake."

From her truck, Ariel snapped on the outside lights and flicked off the alarm.

"So, where do you live?"

"Santa Monica. I own my own condo. Fifteenth floor."

Five minutes later they were sipping Bordeaux in front of a roaring fire. Gas flames. The night had suddenly cleared and the sky was filled with stars. All that was left of the rain was the smell.

Ariel spoke first. Hesitantly. "Soooo...what can I say after seventeen years? I mean...did I do something? You disappeared without a word."

"I tried to keep in touch, Ariel. I wrote you from Alaska when I was ten. A postcard."

"My mother tore it up." Ariel took a step back. "I can't believe you're here, Miranda. My only cousin. Shit, we were born on the same day. We spent every minute of every day together from the time we were babies."

"I know, I know." Miranda's eyes teared up. "Let me take a deep breath. I'll tell you everything. But not this minute. I'd rather look at you." Miranda shook her head. "God, it's like looking in a mirror. We still look...I-DEN-tic-al."

It was true. Except for the hair, they were the same.

"What do you weigh?" Miranda asked.

Ariel stood up. "One-twelve. I gained a lot the first year of the show. We all did. But now I'm back at my perfect weight. How about you?"

"One-ten. I get more exercise than you. Doing porno, you have to be an acrobat."

They laughed together as Ariel pulled Miranda up from the sofa out into the fire light.

"Stand right there," said Ariel, "and let me put on the brights."

"Here?"

"In front of the mirror. By me. Face to face."

They glanced back and forth at their likenesses. Everything was the same except for the hair. They kissed.

"Miranda, my god... Why did it take you so long? You knew I was out there! My face is everywhere. If you'd once called the show or written the studio, I'd have jumped." There were tears in her eyes.

"I know, Ariel. I know. I've spent the last five years trying not to look like you."

They sat down together on the couch. There was an awkward pause.

Ariel finally began. "Alright. So tell me, what is this all about? Why the silence for seventeen years?"

"Have anything stronger than red wine?"

"I got grass." Ariel reached under the couch for the bag Henry had given her. "Want me to roll it for you, or would you like it in a pipe?"

"I don't need it. You do." Miranda watched as Ariel skillfully rolled a joint. A large one wrapped in blue papers. "Okay? You ready?"

Ariel took three hits on the joint. "I'm not sure. I got some coke in the bedroom."

"That would only make it worse."

They sat down together on the couch. Ariel said, "Just tell me what I did wrong. Me or my father or...we're first cousins, for Christ sake." She took a full hit.

"You did nothing, Ariel. Nothing at all. How do I put this..."

"Would you like a whack at this, cuz?" Ariel passed her the grass.

Miranda shook it off. "Firstly, we're not really cousins. Not in the strictest sense."

"What do you mean by that?"

"We're...half sisters." Miranda shook her head and held her breath. "When my father was dying...he confessed to my mother... This is hard for me. He said he had sex with your mom."

"Wait, wait, wait..."

"And...to put it simply, you were his daughter. Your Uncle Bill was really your father. That's what the whole thing was about. My father was your father too. That's why we left."

"Come on."

"Two sisters married two brothers. Only...one brother was father to the both of us. That's what happened. That's what my father told my mother."

"Miranda, this is crazy."

"I know, I know. It sounds crazy, but let me finish. When my dad died, your mother...spoke to..."

"My mother."

"Yes." Miranda was crying. "She told her the whole goddamed thing. How your father couldn't have kids anyway..."

"My god. I never knew that. So that's why you left."

"Yes. You see...we're half sisters, Ariel. Born on the same day. Same father, different mother. Do the DNA. My mother was so mortified."

"My god. Now it all makes sense. No wonder we look like twins."

- 2 -

After they had drunk all the wine, smoked all the grass, eaten the lemon cake, and taken two Seconal each, Ariel and Miranda cried themselves to sleep on the big bed overlooking the Pacific under the painting of a London church done by Ariel's favorite painter, John Piper.

In the morning they took a shower together and marveled at the precise replication of their two bodies.

"We are the same person with different lives," Ariel exclaimed.

"Very different. I have to be at the studio at nine," said Miranda. "Not at all like your studio. Believe me!"

"I don't want this to end, Miranda. We have sooooo much to catch up on. What are you doing tonight?"

"Nothing I can't cancel. Come to *my* place. It's on Fourth Street in Santa Monica, just south of Montana. Top floor. How's nine?"

"Nine is fine. I'll be there on time. What's your condo number?"

"It's the whole top floor."

- 3 -

That evening, the two half sisters caught up on all the life that had flowed away from them since they were eight.

"When you say studio," Ariel began, "what exactly does that mean? The studio I work in has been in business since 1921."

Miranda laughed. "When I say studio, I mean studio. Porno is the number two business in Southern California. Number one is narcotics and number three is you-entertainment."

"Come on." They were lying on the floor of Miranda's sunken living room sipping diet cokes.

"Ariel, look around you. A penthouse apartment with a full view of the ocean from end to end. I drive a Jaguar and you drive a truck. Does this look like poverty? I'm in magazines too." She gave out a wicked giggle. "They get to see more of me. That's all."

"I bet. But listen, I drive a truck because I like trucks, and I went to Yale. I told you. You know how long it takes to get Yale out of your system? It's worse than food poisoning. I have my own production company and I own a ranch. *Both* tax deductible."

"I don't know anything about Yale, but as long as we're getting personal here, how many of those guys on *South Coast* have you slept with? As one sister to another. *My* sex life is well documented. Don't be coy."

Ariel laughed. "All of them except Bruce. And Bruce is fruity."

"You don't say gay?"

"I hate PC. Yale was so PC, you could not say the word *dwarf* there. Besides, Bruce slept with Josh. Bruce told me. Girl to girl."

"No."

"I swear, Miranda. And how many of *your* co-stars have you slept with?"

"Not all of them, that's for sure. I have clauses in my contract..."

"Get outta here." They both began laughing then rolled on the floor. Like teenagers. "You don't sleep with all the guys in porno?"

"I do it for a living, so I get to choose the ones I don't want to fuck. I sleep with girls too and I like it. Not as much as guys, but you get used to it. You're not shocked, are you?"

"No. I saw the film. I mean...that blond guy... How much of *that* is acting?"

"A lot. More than you think! First, there's voiceovers. I mean, they can't stick a mike on you when you're sucking a guy's cock, now can they? Know what I mean?"

"Well..." Ariel was sipping a diet coke. "I can't really imagine what it would be like making love, if that's what you call it, out there under all those lights...I mean doing it out there in front of all those people."

"It's just work. I call it work. You get used to it. It's a job. I have my own suite at the studio, and the money comes in wads. You should see the clothes they give me. I hardly have to shop for anything. The most expensive lingerie you could imagine. Let me show you. We're still the same size, I bet. Want to try some on?"

"I have plenty of lingerie. Believe me. From all my admirers. It's the first thing they bring me after I do them. So, sis? Should I call you sis? That's what we are, aren't we? Sisters?"

"Half sisters. Sure. Call me sis. I have a brother. He's up in Alaska. But you, Ariel...now that I think about it...are my only sister."

"And your stepfather? You said your mother remarried..."

"That's a long story. No, he didn't abuse me, and that's not why I'm in porno. He was kind of a rabbi?"

"Come on."

"No, really. It's a very long story. I'd rather not go into it. It's all very boring. Could you get me a coke?"

Ariel went to the kitchen and opened the fridge.

"God, Ariel. It's amazing! We're both twenty-five years old and famous."

"Sort of. I mean, your life is waaay beyond anything I ever dreamed of at Yale. I'm *so* glad you showed up when you did. My career is stuck to the tube, and *my* life is so fucking boring these days! I've been a high school senior on this goddamn show for five fucking years now, and it's just shit. I've fucked my way through all the guys but Bruce, and the women hate me for it. I could do with a real change. Something new. Here you are showing up just at the right time."

"Oh yeah? What did you have in mind, sis?"

"Well, first of all, I'm not sure I'll ever speak to my mother again."

"Come on. That was a long time ago. I got over it."

"I know," said Ariel, "but I just found out. I thought my dad stole all your money. I thought it was something I did, or my mother or...maybe the day we ruined our shoes. Easter Sunday. Not something like this. No wonder my mother tore up your postcard. What will I say to my father?"

"Nothing. You'll say nothing. He got the business."

"And what was that stuff about Kodiak Island?"

"Leave that for another time." Miranda pulled her long blond hair into an upsweep and posed before her mirror. "So where do we go from here?"

"You tell me," said Ariel, pouting like Tanya in *South Coast*.

"Okay, when do I get to meet Josh Perrin? He already knows about me from my film. He knows what I do."

"And you know him from TV. Meeting Josh can be arranged. Let me think about it. It's kind of a chess move. One thing follows another. I have a really wild idea. I'd like to be blond!"

Ariel put her hands into Miranda's hair.

"Well?" asked Miranda.

"Well, maybe the best way to meet him..."

"Yes."

They were both smiling.

"...is to pretend you're me," said Ariel. "Then you can really get to know him."

"Come on, Ariel."

"I'm serious. First, the blondie will have to go. Then I'll fill you in on the whole goddamn rag bag of cast secrets."

"That'll be fun."

"And I have one little tiny scar on my thigh. You can wear a band aid."

Miranda laughed. "I believe you're serious."

"I am. Know how to drive a truck?"

THREE

Miranda spent her week finishing up *After the Prom*, her 56th porno extravaganza, while Ariel went off to Vegas for a location shoot of *South Coast*. Each was thinking about the other. They talked several times on the phone, always at night.

"Miranda?"

"Ariel, it's three-thirty."

"I know, I know. I couldn't sleep. I've been thinking about you all night."

"I wasn't sleeping much either. I just fell asleep. Are you with Josh?"

"He's zonked. He took sleeping pills. His mother's in town."

"How was the shoot in Vegas?"

"A vice president's wet dream. Soooo, have you been thinking about what I asked you, sis?"

"I was thinking about Josh sleeping with Bruce. That worries me."

Ariel laughed. "Josh is straight all the way. Bruce got him onto the show because his father produces *South Coast*. Goliath Productions. David is his father. It was just a one time thing. Nothing at all. A fantasy favor."

"In my business, Ariel, bi's can be life-threatening."

"Bi's?"

"Bi-sexuals. We don't hire them. Sooooo. Is he next to you?"

"I'm in the den. My den. Groves and Jones can't get onto the property here, remember? Point Dume. A gate and electric fences. Soooo tell me, are you still hung up on Josh?" Ariel gave out a loud giggle.

"Well, I've been thinking about what you said. How you and I are the same person in two separate bodies. I know that's not true, but..."

Miranda heard a dish crash, and then a groan.

"Oh shit!" Ariel exclaimed. "I woke him up. Wait. It's okay, Josh. Nothing. I'm not sick. I'm on the phone with my mother. She can't sleep. Take a lude, okay? Listen, Miranda, Sunday's my day off and *every* Sunday I lease a plane at the airport. Your airport."

"My airport?"

"Santa Monica."

"You have your own pilot?"

"I fly it myself. I have a pilot's license. I'm instrument rated. It's a twin engine Beechcraft B60. Know the Turnaround Café?"

"You mean that restaurant where all the girls line up to meet John Travolta?"

"Yeah. They wish. That's the place. Right out on the runway. I'll meet you there Sunday at noon. Let's talk. I have an idea. Okay, sis?"

"Is it about Josh?"

"Definitely."

"Okay. See you at the Turnaround, sis." Miranda had a little trouble saying that word. Sis. It had a hiss to it. She'd never used it before, not even in porno. She tried to make it sound natural, but it crossed a taboo line. It had all been so sudden. She wanted to be sister close to Ariel, but Miranda wasn't there yet.

"So, I can count on you? Call Nancy if you change your mind."

"I'll be there, Ariel. I'm into the idea of Josh. Should I look for Groves and Jones?" She heard another groan from Josh. "Air, what's goin' on?"

"They follow me every-place. Okay, Josh. I'll bring you some Perrier. I gotta go. He's up."

"I'll wear my dark glasses. I'm a star too, you know."

"You sure are, sis." Ariel hung up the phone and looked at herself in the mirror. "You have no idea, Miranda. You have no idea."

- 2 -

The Turnaround Café is all about ambiance. Tom Cruise pops in regularly and a former president has been seen there many nights on the arm of a famous Hollywood Hostess. The food is just for show.

Miranda had been there before, mostly for drinks. "What's good here?"

"Nothing," said Ariel. "Have a beer. My plane's getting gassed up."

They sat at the bar, both wearing dark glasses.

Miranda kissed Ariel on the cheek, saying, "You don't look happy."

"Fucking studio politics. The year's almost up. That's when the shit piles up."

"By politics, you don't mean Democrats and Republicans?"

"By politics, I mean money. Fucking liberals. I told you, I went to Yale, sis. Yale, where they once hated Jews, blacks, Catholics and queers, and to make up for it *now* they do a complete one-eighty. It's the same in Hollywood."

"Hollywood hated Jews?" They both laughed. Two beers arrived.

"They kiss up to Cardinals and pro-Castro Cubans and Hip Hop pimps. It's just for show." Ariel sipped her beer.

"Hey, be careful. Don't go slandering pimps. They were the founding fathers of porno."

Ariel spat up her beer, laughing. "You're right. I just hate all the politics. And the politicians. I mean, all politicians."

"Me too. I don't see the point of them."

Ariel's cell phone rang. "Drink up, sis. My plane's ready."

They headed from the bar out onto the field.

"How long have you been a pilot?"

"Hold it."

A man in a red jump suit handed her the keys. "She's all gassed up for you, Miss O."

"Thanks, Carl."

"I filed your flight plan." He climbed up the steps beside the plane and opened the door. "Watch the cross winds over Point Magu. Charts are on the seat."

"You're an angel, Carl." Ariel climbed up into the pilot's seat and began to flick switches. She instructed Miranda, "Slam the door, then lock it."

"Wow, this is some plane. How long you been a pilot?"

"Since I was seventeen. My daddy taught me how to fly. He was nice..."

"Is that a tear?"

Ariel choked back a sob. "He was always so good to me. It must have been horrible for him." She put on her headset and revved up the twin engine plane.

At that moment Groves and Jones appeared. Groves pointed to the plane. Ariel spotted them as she taxied down the runway.

"Those guys...are like crib death."

"Where are we going?"

"My hunting lodge."

"CTBX 220, cleared for takeoff."

As she taxied down the runway, Ariel kept her eyes on the dials.

"You're a hunter?"

When they were airborne, Ariel responded. "My daddy taught me to shoot. And to hunt. Hear that, boys. I know how to shoot. He also taught me how to fly. I guess he wanted a son."

Ten minutes later they were soaring up over the ocean, headed north.

"So," said Ariel, banking the plane out up along the coast. "You want to be me for a night? With Josh?"

"I think that was your idea."

"Fucking right. I'm so bored with life and so is Josh. He's thirty-one years old. His sideburns are turning gray and on *South Coast* he's still in high school. Except for the pay, it's like working in a factory. If you could just finish out the year for me."

"Come on, Ariel, I haven't said anything yet!"

Ariel persisted. "First, there's the hair. My girl will do it. Olivia. We'll see if you can fool her."

"I haven't agreed to this yet. It's a big thing to sleep with Josh Perrin, pretending I'm you. It could all go very wrong and wreck my career. I mean, why would you want me to sleep with him?"

"First, there's Groves and Jones. I'd love to fool them. Legally."

Ariel pointed down, dead ahead. "Look out there. That huge place? That's Bruce's beach house."

"Wow. Where are we? Santa Barbara?"

"Ventura. See that van down there?"

"The red one?"

"Guess who? Groves and Jones. They left before I took off! Here we swing east along the highway to Santa Paula. We're an hour ahead of them."

"God, they're like leeches. How did they know where you're going?"

"Once a week I fly up to my ranch." Ariel banked the plane and began to descend. "Okay, sis, so what do you say? How would you like to be Ariel O'Brien? At least for a short time?"

"This is all coming on too fast for me, *sis*. I need to know what I'm getting into before I change my hair to become Tanya, the girl on *South Coast*."

Ariel laughed. After radioing the tower, she said, "That makes sense, but you don't have too long. *South Coast* has a two hour movie coming up this summer. Two weeks away. Every year we shoot it in some exotic place. Last year it was Tahiti. This year it's Malta. I'll be away a month. Starting two weeks from today."

"I can't keep up."

"See those blue buildings on the hill? That's my lodge. Gunslinger Ranch. Two miles from the airport."

"All that land is yours?"

"Yup. It's for hunters." Ariel laughed. "You should hear the stupid cast go off on that one. When I told them I bought a hunting lodge, they went crazy. 'You shoot deer? How terrible. How savage.' " She twisted up her mouth like Anaca James. "Josh has guns all over his house and he won't drive anywhere without his little Beretta, but he didn't say a thing. Just sat there and let them ride me about it."

"KP60 cleared for landing."

"Roger. The studio has guards following them around with Uzis. The Hip Hop guys make kajillions talking about guns. The whole world is crawling with U.S. weapons."

"Okay, okay. Don't get so excited. I get it. If I don't take this job off your hand and sleep with Josh Perrin, you'll shoot me. Man, sis, you *are* tough."

"Right. Let's talk it all out today, you and me. All of it, even if Groves and Jones get some of it on their spy scope. Final approach."

Ariel squealed the landing gear down, guiding the plane onto the runway, without even a bump. "Just a little cross wind. Feel it?"

"Nope. That was perfect. I was nervous when we took off, but you sure know how to fly this fucking thing."

"Thanks. I'm even better with a gun."

- 3 -

Groves and Jones exited the 101 freeway as the Beechcraft descended. A bright sun was high up in the sky, shining directly in their faces. Groves was driving the van. "Who's the blonde?" he asked.

"Don't know, Ray. Didn't get a good look." Jones had on his earphones. "How did the photos turn out?"

"Not good enough. Perrin's got his thumb on her nipple, but her eyes look wrong."

"What do you mean, her eyes look wrong?"

"I mean she doesn't look like Ariel O'Brien. I've got all of her, right down to her very pink clitoris, but the face just doesn't look like her. Si told us to go back again and get it right. 'There's something funny about her eyes,' he said."

"Maybe she was coming. Women never look the same when they're coming," said Bud Jones. "It's the eyes, the way they roll back."

"I did notice one thing. She has a small scar on the inside of her thigh."

"Goes with the hunting and riding. Don't suppose she's going dyke on us, do you? I mean, she carries rocks in her truck, builds her own walls, flies a plane, and shoots jackrabbits. Dyke's not the story we want, is it, Ray?"

"Nope" said Groves. "That would be okay for Rodah Krinkley. Not

25

for Princess Ariel O'Brien, the girl every boy over ten wacks off to in his dreams."

"Including you."

"Including me. We turn off here. Is the antenna up? We should catch some of what they're up to if the sound's on."

- 4 -

It was a cool, suede jacket kind of day in the high desert. Miranda and Ariel spent the afternoon at Gunslinger Ranch shooting jackrabbits, smoking cheroots, and gossiping about the cast and crew of *South Coast*. Ariel stuck to her guns.

"I want you to sleep with Josh. We really dig each other, but I need a change. We both do. I don't want to lose him, sis. He needs me to hold onto, and I need him just to get through the next season. He's my eyes and ears on the show. He makes me laugh. Without him, I'd kill Anaca. I swear. I just need a break and that's where you come in, with your professional skills as Mira Monroe."

"My *professional* skills?"

"As an adult film star. Pull the hammer back. It's single action. For beginners."

They were firing rifles up range into high grass.

"Okay," said Miranda. "Suppose I do this for a week or two. Live your life. What's so important about Josh? What do I need to know, except that I want him all over me?"

Ariel's shotgun banged twice. Two jackrabbits leapt up out of the grass, while a third flipped sideways, dropping softly to the ground.

"Nice shot, sis. Let me get this straight. You want me to be a replacement while you go off and play?"

"I haven't thought that out yet," said Ariel.

"And what about my life? I've got obligations too. I suppose you'll dye your hair blond and become Mira Monroe?"

"I've been thinking about just that. And maybe Josh will figure it out. So what. He loves games. He might get into it. He's the only one on the set who can handle David."

"David?"

"The producer. Brucie's father. David Ivy."

"The bad guy, right," said Miranda.

"No. David is just all there, that's all. He's on it. He's old. Forty. Josh likes him. Josh is his favorite. He lets him direct. Josh wrote the stupid, fucking PC gun show just to make me mad... Without Josh, I'm not making it through one more fucking year of *South Coast*, even if we do graduate this year."

They both laughed.

"So, if you really want to know what I had in mind, Miranda, you're like a summer vacation."

"That's a relief." Miranda raised her gun and fired at nothing. "Tell me about the gun show?"

Ariel spat out her cheroot and cranked off two blasts into a nest of quails. "Fuck the gun show. *South Coast* is soooo boring. Our show this week is about my little brother finding a forty-five in our dad's dresser. A trophy from Vietnam. My kid brother, who's a genius in real life, 190 IQ, he shoots the kid next door by accident. They're arguing right now about whether Clancy should die or not. Clancy's the kid next door."

Miranda laughed. "We don't get into fights like that in the adult film world."

"Not over ten-year-old boys. It's so fucking silly. Two months ago there *was* no little brother. They just invented him. There was no next door. It's so made up. I hate it. Josh keeps me sane. I'm just tired of fucking him. You do it, Miranda. You fuck him for me. I'm signing him over to you."

"You want me to fuck the sexiest guy on TV? Alright. I'll do it. I'll fuck him for you. How tough can that be? It's not like I don't do it all the time, right?"

"For a living. Look over there." Ariel pointed to a glint at the top of the rise. "See that piece of glass on top of the rock? Hand me your rifle." Ariel focused her 6X sight. "Now you look."

"I see it, okay? It's glass."

"Fire at it. See how close you can get to the reflection."

"What is it? A mirror?"

"Just shoot. It's on my property!"

Miranda took aim, cocked the single action thirty-thirty, firing one, then another round.

The first one struck the rock where Groves was listening in. The retort second shot knocked the recorder out of Bud Jones's hand.

"Not a bad shot," said Ariel. "I think you hit something. Maybe Groves and Jones."

"I hope you're kidding."

"I'm not kidding. They're on my property. Now how about Josh? Do you want to sleep with Josh, pretending to be me?"

"Maybe for a few days."

"Not good enough. I need a real commitment."

"Okay. Absolutely. One actress playing the other. I've fantasized about him so long, the idea of really fucking him makes me come in my pants. He's so goddamn perfect. I mean, how do you stand it working with him on the set every day?"

"You get used to it. Like you, fucking women. Now let's see if you can hit that van parked up there under the trees on private land. My land."

"I'm not into killing people, Ariel. Not even if they work for *Flem*."

"I am," said Ariel. She wasn't smiling. "Hungry? We only serve steaks at Gunslinger. Blood meat. Hunter's kill. That's the way I like mine. Bloody. How about you, sis? Don't say medium."

Miranda hated meat. All meat. She preferred pasta or rice, but she left her culinary tastes unspoken for Josh Perrin's sake. Josh was the meat she really wanted.

"There are only two ways to eat steaks," Ariel continued. "Bloody or burnt black. There is no medium when it comes to meat, or life either. Which way do you like yours?"

"Black as coal," lied Miranda. "We can't be the same in everything."

- 5 -

On the flight back to L.A. Ariel was all revved up. She had what she wanted from Miranda and her mind went racing ahead. "Our accents are almost the same," she said. "Watch out for *water*. I'm still Southern Connecticut and your *New* York is a little too Alaska for me. *Watter* is where I'm at."

"I noticed that. *Watter*. How's that?"

"Good. Josh would recognize your *Yurk*. He has perfect pitch. Josh can tell Vaughn Monroe from Matt Monroe in just two notes. He's an expert on Forties music. You have to know that about him. And he sings. Baritone. Perfectly. I'll tell you all of it, everything you want to know about Josh Perrin, but first I need you to dye your hair black. Olivia does my hair. I want you to be me for Olivia. Show up just as you are. Tell her I'm up for a part as Jean Harlow. That's why the hair is platinum blond. Rush job. She'll bitch. She hates it when anyone else does my hair. Olivia's a great place to start. You'll have to convince her you're me. See if she buys it. If you fail with Olivia, you'll fail with Josh."

Miranda was beginning to enjoy losing control of her life. "What the hell, if she finds out? She's a hair dresser."

Ariel laughed. "Look down there. There's the Biltmore Montecito. Josh took me there last month for my birthday. Our birthday."

They laughed together.

"Hate to tell you, but I've been there too, sis." Miranda hissed out the last *S*. "A one night stand, two months ago with someone famous. Can't say who, but you've heard of him. Sooooo, Sisssss, tell me more about Josh Perrin. All about him. What does he like in women? How is he in bed?"

"There's one more detail. I think I told you."

"What's that?"

"I have a scar on my right thigh. Two inches long and straight. Josh calls it my runway. You'll need to cover up that part of your thigh."

"How would I do that?"

"Put a bandage over it. One that won't come off. Tell him you're having plastic surgery. We talked about it once or twice. He told me I should get a tattoo there. He has one on his butt. And shave your pubic hair. Take every hair of it off. Josh is totally cunt crazy. He wants nothing in the way."

"Cunt crazy? That's a little vulgar, even for a Yalie. You mean he's girl crazy!"

"I mean he's cunt crazy. There's no other way to say it. What makes Josh Perrin's engine run is the all-American, hairless snatch. Forget the rest of the body when it comes to Josh. If you have purple nipples like me, he'll notice them, but to him they're just a conversation piece. Josh has non-stop porno going day and night at his place, and it's all about what's at the fork in the road between the thighs."

Ariel dipped the wing of her plane and descended down over the Channel Islands. Then she shot the plane up into an almost vertical climb. "Feel that, sis?"

"Jeeez, Ariel, how can you do that after a two pound bloody steak?"

"Trying to get your attention. With Josh...you need to understand the man. At last count, Josh has slept with four hundred eigthy-seven females and one male. He's taken photos of every woman he's ever slept with."

"Even you?"

"Especially me."

"So you think taking pictures is gonna bother me?"

"Just pictures of your *cunt*. Got it? He has them arranged by color from pink to deep carmine. He knows them by sight, every one. He'll show you. The names are on the back. He's memorized the color of each labia, the shape of every clit. But the inside stuff is what really gets him off. He knows it all by touch and smell. Like a blind man knows his gloves."

"Come on. This is all about--"

"Pussy. And he knows it best by taste. Is it salty or bitter, or oily or creamy, or does it taste like roast beef?"

"You're scaring me."

"He'll eat you for an hour just using the tip of his tongue, until your womb crawls out and swallows up his head."

"You're making me wet."

"He's studied Tantra sex in India, and he knows more than most of his teachers. He's had more experience. He can talk about the clitoris for hours. The tough ones, the smooth ones, the soft ones, the ones with the hooded eye."

"He seems so cool on TV."

"He is cool on TV." Ariel radioed in her approach and released the landing gear.

"Come on, Air. He can't be that crazy. How the fuck does he learn his lines?"

"Josh reads them once and he's got it down. There's the Point Dume Club."

"I mean, how about my ass? I have a goddamned beautiful ass."

"Just cunts. He knows all the women he's been with by the way their pussy smells. Anaca, he says smells like smoked salmon. He told me I smell and taste like caviar. His favorite scent is liver. I forget who smells like liver. And he'll talk about juices. He even likes it when I'm bloody and in full flow. He's all over me when I'm on my third day. He'll stick his thumb right up into Wonderland, as he calls it, and scoop out a whole thumb of catsup squirt."

"*Jeeez!* You're scaring me. He sounds totally crazy."

"Cunt crazy. That's what I said. He's absolutely *cunt* crazy. Fifty-four K to tower."

"Cleared for approach, cunt crazy."

"Oh jeez, I'm sorry."

"Don't even think about it. This is Santa Monica. Over."

Miranda giggled. So it was going to happen. She and Josh Perrin. "And what do I need to know about the cast? I'll have to fool them too."

"That's another four hours. Stay over tonight. I'll fill you in on everything. I'll even lend you my lingerie. No offense, but the stuff you wear would throw him off."

"Okay."

"See that plane? The one coming in ahead of us? It belongs to Tom Cruise."

"Man, it's been a day, Ariel."

"Call me Air. That's what my friends call me. Ariel is too much Shakespeare."

As the Beechcraft gently touched the tarmac, Ariel's thoughts went racing ahead. In her mind, Miranda had already become her understudy and *South Coast* was fading fast.

"Jeez, Air, you bring it in so smooth."

Carl was waiting. He opened the door.

The sun was just going down.

- 6 -

"Your eye's all black, Ray."

"Is there any more blood?"

Bud Jones looked in the rear view mirror. "I washed it all off. Are you sure the bullet didn't hit you?"

"I think they used shotguns."

"We better stop and have it looked at."

"On a Sunday? I'll take my chances. A little whiskey might help."

"You could charge her, you know. If it was me, Ray, I'd call out the sheriff."

"We were trespassing on her land. The blonde did it. A.O. might a hired her to kill us. Her shot bounced off the dish. Plumb luck."

Jones passed him a bottle of Jack Daniels, first taking a swig and splashing a shot or more onto his shirt sleeve. He dabbed the liquor onto Grove's cheekbone, just below the right eye.

"Does it sting?" Jones asked.

"Shit yeah," said Groves. "It stings like a sonofabitch."

FOUR

"So you got by Olivia, I hear?" Ariel was on the floor of Miranda's bedroom, doing leg pulls, watching the new video, *After the Prom*. She studied the way Miranda moved her hips as the Blond Bazooka banged her from behind.

"How do you know that?" Miranda stared down at Ariel, chewing an apple.

"She called me and asked why I didn't just wear a wig for the Harlow part."

Miranda laughed. "What did you tell her?"

"Next time. Now there's Nancy. She knows about you, but I want you to fool her too. Like Olivia. She knows me better than anyone."

"Better than Josh?" Miranda licked her lips.

"Better than Josh. Josh has one thing on his mind. The inner woman. That's all. Nancy knows my bank accounts, my income tax, my bar bills, where I go when I have VD."

"Come on. You mean you've had VD?"

"Every actress in Hollywood has had at least one case of the clap. It's job related. About Nancy. She has a few quirks. Likes to say *chinga* and I always make a face. Then there's coffee. I drink it black *unless* I'm hung over. Then I take skim milk. And she can always tell when I'm getting my monthlies. I start to tear up. Okay. Inspection."

"How do I look?"

They were facing Miranda's gold mirror.

"You look just like me." Ariel gave Miranda's cheek a pat. "Like Ariel O'Brien. Star of *South Coast*. Tanya to her fans. So...what do you need?"

"Should I take your license? Just in case? I'm driving your truck."

"Good idea." Ariel reached down into her bag and fumbled through her wallet. "How about my Visa card? Just in case. My Triple A and my library card. You never know when you might want to check out a book." She dropped a stack of cards, bound by a rubber band, into Miranda's upraised palm. "Now give me yours."

"You don't even look like me."

"Not yet, but look, I'm giving you Josh Perrin. The fuck of the century."

Miranda gave her wallet to Ariel. "Take it all, porno queen."

Miranda laughed, stealing one more glance at the mirror. "Okay. I'm ready. My keys are on the dining room table. My place is your place, sis. You can be Mira Monroe as long as you like." She planted a kiss on Ariel's cheek, then trotted for the elevator.

Ariel held her breath. She watched from behind the curtains as Miranda slammed the door of her truck, started up the engine and drove off.

"Step one," said Ariel to the empty street below. "Gajesus."

Close behind Miranda, in their red van, were Groves and Jones. Everything was going perfectly.

- 2 -

The truck was automatic, no problem. Miranda zipped up Seventh Street, then down and around Santa Monica Canyon. She laughed at Ariel's thoroughness. They'd compared perfumes and deodorants. Ariel had tasted her breath with a mock soul kiss. She checked the bandage on her left leg, then shaved off all the pubic hair on her pussy, spreading the labia, inspecting deep inside with a flashlight and a mirror.

"Pinkish rose," Miranda recalled her saying. "Almost a perfect match."

"Why almost?"

"You have a few steak lines running east west."

"Steak lines? I do?"

"Josh calls them that. He has this thing about meat."

"I bet."

"Henry will give you some grass. Make Josh smoke it before you drive home."

"Oh, Henry. He's..."

"Pat's Secretary of Agriculture. He likes me."

Traffic was light on PCH. The moon was bright and high in the sky as Miranda pulled up into the drive at the Dublin Club.

Henry was waiting outside. "You're late, Miss A. He's been here twenty minutes."

According to Ariel, she was right on time. To the minute.

"Here's your little package." Henry handed her a white paper bag. "Paid for."

Pat was standing in the doorway. Pat, the putative Irishman. Miranda had met him once before. One of her famous "dates" had taken her there for a drink.

"Princess," he gushed. "So wonderful to have you both under my roof again."

"Where we belong." As Mira Monroe, she was ignored. Now, as Ariel O'Brien, proprietor Pat pressed his heavy bulk up against her breasts.

"I put you back in the corner." He pointed to the darkest spot in the club. Josh wasn't there. "He's at the bar." Pat pointed.

Josh Perrin was dressed in black. Miranda wore a dark red dress and matching heels. Her neckline scooped low and her skirt length was high. She wore the ruby necklace Josh had given Ariel on their second date.

"Air, you look so..." He snatched her ass gently and whispered, "edible."

"I'm dessert." She was nervous. Pat hovered in their vicinity, showing them off to his patrons. So much for anonymity.

"Enrique. Their table." He pointed to the back of the room. "The Fenns are not here tonight."

"Too bad," said Josh. "Enrique, two Brandy Alexanders."

"Of course."

"You look delish." As Josh bent down to catch the ruby pendant with his fingers, he kissed Miranda on the nose, then ran his tongue along her lips. Miranda shuddered.

Josh smiled. Miranda caught her breath. Josh Perrin had his hand on her both breasts, moving from left to right.

"Be coy," Ariel had said. "Just pretend you're Tanya."

"Josh." Miranda removed his hand as it slid down along her dress. They both sat down. Enrique brought their drinks. Miranda had never had a Brandy Alexander. She was pleased with the taste. Milky sweet. She was cool with Josh even though her heart was pounding like a broken water pump.

"So what's in the bag?" he asked.

"Something from Henry. Agricultural."

"Oh, yeah. Good. Perfect for Tantra. Sooo, Air, ready for Malta?"

"No." She gave him the Tanya pout, the one she'd seen on *South Coast* from the first episode. The one that made Ariel O'Brien a household name.

"Why the funny face?"

"I don't want to go when you're totally not going."

"I thought we talked that all out. I have a film gig." Josh seemed annoyed.

Miranda felt nervous. They drank their Brandy Alexanders in silence. Patrons were gawking. Josh kept his eyes on Miranda, staring at her left ear. Was it the earrings? She gave him a quizzical look.

"Olivia cut your hair too short," said Josh. "Just above the ear. I'll have a word with her."

"You'll do no such thing. I don't talk to..." And then she stopped.

"Charles." Josh laughed. "You always forget his name. God, Ariel, you do look hot tonight."

"I am hot."

They sailed through the salad and the medallions of beef, talking of Malta.

Miranda did her best. She had out her fake book. "They speak English there, you know." At least she knew that. "And I think Ulysses was marooned there."

"Oh, is that right? Taking your instrument?"

That one threw her. "Maybe," was all she said.

By the time dessert arrived, Josh had downed two Brandy Alexanders and three double scotches. He'd dropped a tab of acid and smoked up all the grass in the men's room.

As he dabbled with his spoon, Miranda put on her porno face, blew him a kiss, and mimicked an orgasm. As Josh reached for his lighter, Miranda popped a Viagra into his spumoni. She was taking no chances.

Josh paid the bill. Pat made a big show for the patrons. "I always love it when you two are in here. You brighten up the night."

Miranda groaned. Not as Mira Monroe, she thought. What a chump.

Pat saw them out into the darkness. Josh was staggering.

"I'd better drive," Miranda whispered.

Josh agreed. "Don't need another DUI with Groves and Jones out there. Pat can hide away the Mas. Right Pat?" Josh dropped the key into his right palm.

"Anything you say. I love you two like children." He gave them each a kiss.

"I'm riding with the trucker, tonight. Your place."

"My place." Miranda agreed.

Josh climbed in on the passenger side and pulled out a Robusto. "Know something, Air, you smell different tonight. I don't know what it is."

"You got me so excited when you ate your ice cream." She popped the key into the ignition, jammed the truck into gear, and shot them out onto PCH with a jagged squeal.

"You see the van?" Josh puffed on his cigar as Miranda scanned the rear view mirror.

"The fuckers. They're right behind us."

A few minutes later, they were in bed. Miranda had on her slip. Josh was in his briefs. Josh started very slowly, as Ariel said he would. *Tantra.* As Miranda sank down into the lavender silk sheets, she reached for the light switch. Just to tease him. To see what Josh would do.

"You are crazy tonight!" Josh exclaimed. "I want them all on. Always. What's the matter with you tonight? I *never* fuck in the dark. How long have we fucked? Five years? *Even after all that time* I still want to see and taste and touch every part of you, O'Brien. Inside and out!"

"Tantra," she said.

"Yes. Slooooow. Tantra."

As he kissed the length of her long black hair, Miranda began to shudder.

"Wild apples," he said.

She longed to speak his name, Josh Perrin, but a pant was all that came out.

"I love your hair. The way it smells like apples." He dipped his tongue into the valley of her part, slowly moving down along her scalp till he reached her brow.

Miranda made a futile grab for his penis, already rigid, but he slapped her hand away. "You *are* overeager tonight, Miss Air. It must be the mussels. Let it go. You know I like it slooooooow. Even when I'm hard. Climbing the mountain begins at the bottom. What's this?" He touched the bandage on her right thigh.

"A tattoo. They went too deep."

"I thought you hated tatoos."

"It's to cover my scar." She knew she should not have said that. She began to shudder as Josh tasted first one eyebrow, then the other, her mascara running down his lips.

"God, god, god." Miranda's throat had gone dry.

"Slow down. Slow down."

"You've got me so fucking hot tonight. Gajesus." An Ariel touch.

Josh kissed both her nostrils, and sucked her nose up into his mouth so hard she couldn't breathe. When he kissed her eyes, softly at first, licking her eyelids shut, she felt a sudden turmoil stirring in her womb and her labia closed down tight upon his thumb.

"Are you all right? You never did that before." He pulled out his thumb and sniffed it.

Miranda held back a scream. "It's just so good. I don't know why I'm so excited."

"I thought you were bored?" Josh licked her neck and chin.

"It makes me shake when you do that."

"Your breath tastes like Russian apples." He slid his tongue along the inside of her ears until he could taste the wax inside, and then he licked the roundness of her ear lobes.

Miranda could hardly breathe as he tongued her throat with a slow, controlled softness. How did he keep his tongue so wet, she thought?

As he held her lips between his fingers, opening them wide, kissing them both with the tip of his tongue, she began to gasp.

"Your breath is so sweet," he said. "I'd like to eat your teeth."

That made Miranda laugh. She rose up and went on the attack, pushing her tongue down his throat as Josh removed her coal black slip.

Miranda still had on her panties and everything inside them churned with passion as she sunk her nails into the tan line on his neck.

"God, you're boiling hot," he said.

"My ovaries are jumping sideways."

"Go slow, Air-e-al. Slow down." He sucked her tongue back down his throat. "You're certainly *not* yourself tonight."

"Josh, wait..."

He felt her where it mattered. "Hot soup," he said.

"I can't control myself. I feel all undiscovered."

"Just slow down." Josh thumbed her nipples and Miranda's heart was pounding harder than a jackhammer. She could feel his cock upon her thigh hard as a tire iron.

"Don't touch," he said.

"Oh, now, Josh. Now." She hung her breasts down over him.

"Tantra," he said. "I've just begun." He sucked her right breast down into his mouth and held it hard against the base of his throat, slowly letting it retract.

"Please, Josh, let me."

"No." He slapped her again.

Then she kissed him until he couldn't breathe.

"Your nipples are hard as purple pebbles. I've always imagined Snow White had nipples just like yours."

"Let me suck you."

"Not yet. I need some blood."

He bit her left breast hard until it bled and the blood ran down his chin.

That slowed Miranda down. That kind of biting was new to her. Blood was forbidden in the porno she did. Spanking was fine, spanking was fun, but there could be no blood. Ariel had not mentioned biting! Bite marks were bad for adult film stars.

Still, the bite excited her, and as Josh reached her navel and tongued it inside out, Miranda began to lose control. Her juices were flowing like a river and she started to come uncontrollably.

"Air, for god's sake get a grip."

"It's the biting. I just let go."

"Okay. No harm done. Come as much as you want, but let's have some focus here. Tantra."

"Tantra," she said, catching her breath as a wave of orgasm pulled at her vulva.

"My, my, my," he said. "So soon."

"You smell like sunshine, Josh."

She bit at his tongue as he slipped her panties off, slowly, gently, moving up into Wonderland.

"Remember," Ariel had warned her, "Josh is absolutely cunt crazy. That's the core of him. He can't get enough labia lunch. And he likes violence."

Miranda tore off his briefs with her teeth.

"Not yet."

"I just want to hold it."

"No," he said as he inspected her sex. "Your pube looks irritated here."

"I'm still a little raw from shaving."

"You don't say." Josh bounded up out of bed heading for the bathroom, returning with two vials of oil and bottle of baby powder.

"Let's put a little softness here." He drew her vortex up to him and ran his tongue along the hood of her clitoris. Then he sprinkled baby powder over the area she and Ariel had recently shaved.

"Taste." Josh daubed a splash of the dark brown oil on his index finger, reaching out to cover both her nipples. "Vitamin E and vanilla extract." He tongued her left nipple like a cat lapping cream, and then he pushed her head down till she could suck her own breast.

"Well?" he asked.

"*Mmmmm.* Not just vanilla. What is that?"

"Secrets of the East. Healing and fattening."

He oiled her clit with the pale yellow vial, and her limbs began to go numb.

"What the hell is that?" asked Miranda. "Liquid Novocain?"

"Close. It'll slow you down. Now let's have a look inside."

As he drew up her open pink vulva, flower fresh and ready, Miranda settled back on the pillows and began to relax into the bio-chemistry of sex. Her mind fell back into the recesses of dreams and memory and fantasy.

Josh Perrin's breath came hot upon her labia. He groaned and panted as if he were breathing in her womb, all of it. She hoped for his sake that she smelled like the douche she had scented herself with a few hours before, rather than the primal scent of raw oysters or roast beef or calves liver. Once, in a porno film, she sucked a woman's cunt until she felt her coming on her tongue and the other actor smelled just like cooked bacon.

Josh drew her thighs up to look down into the cave markings and striations and colorations of her inner cunt, and his eyes glazed over as though he'd taken opium.

"Air, what's this? Up here it's creamy white."

"My juices are flowing so hard."

As he opened her and peered deep down into her womb, Josh had the vague sensation something was not the same. Foggy on grass and al-cohol and designer drugs, he spelunked inward, tasting and touching and breathing in the inner parts of her sexual geography, all so familiar to him, yet something was dissimilar, something was not quite the same. There was an extra line of latitude to her that he had never seen before. Or was he just crazy? Cunt crazy?

Great wine tasters have the knack to recognize what others miss in fine wines. Josh Perrin was a taster of cunts. The best. The most skilled. He used touch and taste and scent as though he were a scientist studying the female sex, and yet, tonight, there was something different about the girl he'd been in love with for years. They'd fucked for five years. Ever since the first day on the pilot of *South Coast*. But tonight Ariel seemed different.

As Miranda swallowed the head of his dick between her lips and licked it with fury, Josh had a wild thought, but he let it pass.

It was Miranda's turn now. She was thoroughly aroused! Had Ariel ever been so hot with him? It was time to let her vadge implode as he sank his nose down between the two pink labia, still childlike and soft, though he'd fucked her more than five hundred times.

"I love the way you taste," she panted. "Like tapioca."

He laughed, then breathed her labia into his mouth like two pieces of pastrami, slowly spitting them out.

Miranda was now on fire as she held his penis in her mouth, and he swallowed up the salt of her clitoris. Raw oysters.

Miranda moaned and squirmed and came again as Josh smacked her on the ass.

"Don't race ahead," he said. "It's not tantric."

"You've been in there so long doing tongue exercises, I got tired of waiting."

He placed her ass up on the pillow, still drunk with the colors of her vulva, then slowly entered her. He could feel her shuddering deep inside as the fist of her cunt clamped down on him and grabbed him with its spasms.

"Talk to me," he said.

- 3 -

"What do you see?" Jones was on the roof of the van, manipulating the sound dish.

"Are you kidding? The lights are on and I'm getting everything. I can't believe they let us in. Right through the fucking gate. How's the sound?"

"She's not talking much. Not as much as she usually does. I think they're really loaded, if he left his car tonight."

"Man, you should see this. It's like they're doing it for the camera."

- 4 -

At five a.m. Ariel called Miranda, saying, "I'm sick, sis. I have a fever. Go in for me. It's just Monday readings."

"Are you sure?"

"I'm sure. Is Josh there?"

"Yeah. He's wasted."

"Fix him two coddled eggs and jump in the limo. Leave the truck. You'll do fine with the readings. I'll stay at your place. Don't talk to Nancy. Got it?"

"Sure. I'll stay off the phone."

FIVE

"That was a night, O'Brien. I can hardly open my eyes."

It was 6:00 a.m., Monday morning. They were racing up Sunset toward the 405 in a limo with a license plate that read PHLUK. Miranda was putting on her mascara as Josh sipped black coffee. "I got two hours sleep, Perrin. Just wanted you to know. How do I look?"

"Which end should I took at?"

"Funny."

"You always look great. Even when you're wasted. On both ends." He glanced down at her legs. "Have you found your cousin yet?"

"I'm working on it." Miranda didn't miss a beat. "Pour me out a cup of that."

"Yeah." Josh checked his watch as they rolled through the studio gates. 6:38 a.m. "God, I hate these hours. I'm so fucking bored with *South Coast*. How can you stand it?"

Miranda held back her answer. It was her first day on the set.

- 2 -

As Josh disappeared into the lighting booth, Miranda was whisked to her dressing room. Before she could close the door, the phone rang. It was Ariel.

"Just remember what I told you. Monday is run through. No makeup, no wardrobe. Olivia will pop in to smooth out your hair."

"And..." Coffee arrived with a light knock.

"*And* you read and listen. David does all the talking. I always sit between Josh and Roger. Watch out for Anaca. Don't get near her. Everything you ever read about the two of us hating each other is true. Don't even look at her. Just read the script and ask a few questions. You know how stupid the show's become. David will walk off the blocking. You obviously know all about camera angles. The tight shot, the slow turn. You do it in porno. Besides, you can act, Miranda. You really can. This is your big chance, spouting a line without some guy's cock in your mouth. True?"

Miranda laughed. "Should I take my coffee black?"

"*Yes.* And don't talk to Nancy when she calls. We have to work on her. At this stage, she'll see right through you. Don't answer the phone at all. My father might call. I mean, my legal father."

Miranda changed the subject. "What does David look like?"

"He's the fat little guy with glasses A five by five."

"Got it. So what the hell do I do in here till they call me?"

"Read my fan mail. The pile labeled 'life threatening'. That could keep you awake all night, okay?'

"Okay." They hung up at the same time.

Miranda found the stack of mail marked TURN OVER TO SECUR- ITY. She opened a large orange envelope and read:

Dear Ariel,

I can't stop thinking about you. Could I have your address?
I keep dreaming of you sleeping with my husband. He knew you at Yale.
He still has a Tampax you gave him when you were 19. Could you please send us a picture of you in the shower with Josh. We know you two are doing it.

Love, Valerie Hottsun. My husband is Paul.

Attached was a photo of the Hottsuns standing naked in their patio holding a black toy poodle.

"Everybody on set," came the announcement.

- 3 -

Ariel turned over in bed and was sinking back to sleep when the phone rang. She'd almost forgotten where she was, and *who* she was.

"Ever heard of French Frigate Shoals?"

"Excuse me, who is this?"

"Who else would it be? Moe."

"Oh, Moe, sorry. I just took a shower and I have water in my ears. No. I've never heard of French Frigate Shoals It sounds like a Carlsbad marina with condos."

Moe laughed. "You must have had a long night."

"Just me and my vibrator. So what's this all about?"

"Your next film. I mean after *Professor Max*. Mr. I's lost love film."

"*Professor Max.* Oh, that one." Ariel was clueless.

"This week. You're her. Stu's wife?"

"Right, Moe."

"You sound funny, Mira. Keep a stiff upper lip under your slip. Stu's motto. Then comes the big one. *Wet Hawaii*. Three weeks from Friday. We're shooting it on French Frigate Shoals. A place no one gets to without pull. Northwestern Hawaii. The boss knows someone high up in the coast guard. Someone big. A general, so we got permission to use it for our film. Mira?"

"Yeah, I'm here. A big shot in the coast guard is maybe an admiral, or a commander. I dated a guy in the coast guard when I was at Yale." It just slipped out.

"You were at Yale?"

"For a very short time."

"You sound funny, Mira. Are you sick?"

"I just woke up."

"You recall the film where we *used* all those Marines still in boot camp? What was it called? *Hard Service*? You said you liked their spontaneity, remember? Are you there? Help me out here, Mira. You lived with one of those fucking Marines for a month, remember? Are you dead?"

"I'm still here." Ariel was quickly filling in the blanks.

"Good. Stu is taking all the girls to Hawaii and just one guy. Me. Mr. Comedy Cock. The rest he's getting from the coast guard. Right out of boat training. Sound like fun to you?"

"Sure."

"He showed me digitals of the place. You won't believe it. We fly over in his private jet with a night or two on Lanai. Drinking and fucking and shooting film. How good does that sound, Mira?"

To Ariel it sounded tempting. To Ariel it sounded anonymous, away from *South Coast*, Josh, David, Inga, Bruce, and Anaca. Even Groves and Jones. To Ariel it sounded heavenly.

"One question, Moe. How would they like it if I showed up as a brunette?"

"I don't think so, beautiful. Mira Monroe is Mira Monroe. Can't mess with the image. It took Stu two years to build it up."

"I know all about images, Moe," Ariel said. "See you soon."

- 4 -

Meanwhile, Miranda was trying to follow the plot line for her role. Holly, played by Inga, was breaking up with Rod, played by Bruce. Best friends Jenny, played by Anaca, and Tanya, Ariel's role, were poised to stop them. Josh was not in the scene. Josh was still getting over the dead kid next door. Josh had tuned out.

The cast was seated in a circle. Miranda did a quick one-eighty. Ten spoiled actors, all in their late twenties or early thirties, stuck in a high school melodrama, trying to look like teenagers. She had to laugh.

"Just read the line, Miss James."

"You are *so* who you are," hissed Anaca.

Miranda gave her a stare. "Sometimes things just go on too long."

"There's no *just*," hissed Anaca.

Ariel had filled Miranda in on the problem. Best friends Jenny and

Tanya hated each other from the first day they worked together. First year, third episode, when Anaca replaced Ariel's real best friend, Bonnie Blair, the girl who got her the role to begin with. Now Bonnie was on Broadway, *starring* as "Miss Julie."

For Ariel O'Brien and Anaca James, cast as best friends who trusted each other with everything, it was a match made in hell. That hatred that began in the beginning was now five years down the road and it had turned to poison.

"Come on, ladies," said David. "Let's get it done. Lunch is almost served."

Mirada read her line. "Things go on too long sometimes."

"Not right." David was irritated. "Try it again. It's flat. Anaca!"

"You *are* so who you are."

"Things go on too long sometimes."

"No. Awful. Let's get it up on its feet." The cast was bored. David rose to his full height of five one. Mister five by five they called him behind his back. "Stand up and face each other."

Anaca shook her head. Miranda was thinking to herself, *I'm an actor playing an Actor. How would Ariel handle this one?*

"I want you close," said David. "Hug."

The cast started giggling. "*Oooh, hhhoooo, hhhoooo,*" laughed Bruce. Josh held his breath.

As Anaca touched Miranda's shoulder with her sharp nails, Miranda felt her knees shake.

"Cunt," Anaca whispered, loud enough so everyone could hear.

Miranda ignored her. "Do I turn here, David?"

"No. Just hug her, release her, and say your line."

"You are *so* who you are...bitch."

"Things go on so long sometimes."

Anaca waited for a response, but nothing happened.

"I need real warmth here girls. Holly and Rod are breaking up. Best friends to the rescue." The cast was smirking. "Nail it ladies."

Miranda glared at Anaca till Anaca backed away.

"David, it's only a run through," said Miranda. "I don't feel it. The line is...I don't know."

David persisted. "I need to see some warmth here."

"Okay." Anaca took a deep breath, thrusting her face four inches from Miranda's glare. Ice against ice. "You are so who you are."

The warmth was wrapped in battery acid, but it worked.

Miranda stood her ground. "Things go on so long sometimes." She said it with real emotion, then reaching out to Anaca, she kissed her on the lips. Hard. The whole cast exploded into laughter.

Anaca James backed off spitting. "Don't *ever* do that again, you fucking cunt. "

David was pleased. "Very good. Let's break for lunch."

- 5 -

"So what do you have for me, Groves?"

"You won't believe it, Mr. I."

"Try me."

"We got the shots. Twenty-five of them. Josh Perrin and Ariel O'Brien. Everything. Audio too."

"Let me see."

Groves handed over the digitals.

"Fucking amazing. Perfect! You can really see it's them. No doubt about it this time."

- 6 -

Doing what Ariel told her, Miranda ducked calls from Nancy Ruiz all afternoon. At four p.m., Miranda called Ariel. "Nancy called five times."

"I know. It's okay. I called her from my cell phone. She thinks we're on location. How was your day?"

"Crazy, but I liked it. I kissed Anaca."

"Wonderful. Fucking wonderful. I hope she still hates me."

"Worse than ever. How was your day?"

"I talked to Moe about your next film, *Professor Max*. I told him you went to Yale."

Miranda laughed. "Speaking of which, I read that letter from Mrs.

Hottsun."

"Yeah, yeah, yeah. Paul was an old flame. He dropped out of Yale and ended up in the service. Look, Mira, we have to talk. I know almost nothing about *your* life. Could I see you, pronto? Say tonight? I have an idea."

"Me too. Where should I meet you?"

"Santa Monica Airport. I'll take you up on a night flight. I'm leaving your place now. I'll lock it up. Where's Josh?"

"He headed off on an audition. He already has the part locked up, he said, but this is Hollywood. How about eight p.m.?"

"Eight is great. Thanks for giving me a day off, Miranda."

"No problem. That's what sisters are for."

As Ariel drove off in the Jag to get her hair dyed blond, and not by Olivia, Miranda took the limo back to Point Dume.

SIX

"Soooooo, he winked at me," said Miranda. "As you."

Ariel laughed. "He's an actor and I'm an actor. And we're both pilots."

"He licked his lips."

"What can I say? He's married."

They were twenty miles out over the Pacific Ocean and it was midnight. The stars were out and there was no moon. According to the KLN94 color GPS with Moving Map, they were heading straight for Japan. Ariel put the plane on auto pilot and took off her head gear.

"Let's go back into the galley and have some sherry," said Ariel. "I need you to tell me everything about adult entertainment. Everything about Mira Monroe and who her friends are. I need to know what it means to be a porno star."

"You're just gonna let the plane fly itself?"

"That's what auto pilot is. Major airlines have it."

"On major airlines someone is always in the cockpit. A co-pilot or something."

Ariel gave her Yale laugh, a chortle followed with a low snort. "This is not a major airline. Miranda, I trusted you with Josh. I gave you the fake book on my life, and I know almost *nothing* about you. This plane has a Multi-Hazard Awareness System, Collision Avoidance alarms, Vertical Profile Color Radar, an Enhanced Ground Proximity Warning System, and Flight Directed Autopilot. Any aircraft within ten miles of us sets off a warning. Look at the flashing lights. You sleep with guys who've had hundreds of sexual partners and don't trust *my* judgment? I mean, who's the risk taker here? You or me, *Miranda*?"

Miranda took a deep breath. "Ariel, I *do* trust you. It's just...I mean, your life is not mine."

"That's for sure. My life is not yours, but I want to try it out for the summer. No Groves and Jones for a change. Take off your safety belt." Ariel opened the cabin door. "Coming?"

"You're sure we're okay?"

"Josh and I once fucked for an hour with the plane on auto pilot. Come on." Ariel pulled Miranda up from her seat and led her back into the cabin of the plane.

Two tables, ten seats, a galley, and lots of teak wood. They sat down together at a table.

"Now sis, let's get serious," said Ariel. "Tell me everything about the world of X rated films." She poured out two glasses of sherry. "You sure fooled Carl. I was certain he'd pick up a trace of your accent."

"Who's Carl?"

"Carl. He gassed up the plane. Same guy as last time."

"This is all happening a little too fast for me, *sister*." Miranda took a tiny sip of her sherry.

"*South Coast* is scary, right?"

"It's not just that. You're asking me to trade my life for yours. I like my life. I like what I do. It took me a long time to get where I am. Do you know they sell my panties right off the set to collectors? Comes with a photo of me and my co-star. They go for a grand each and I get half. And the photo goes directly into the magazine."

"Which magazine is that?"

"Look, *sis*, a few things are off limits here. Like my IRS statements. I can't tell you everything, Ariel. I'll tell you what you need to know. My hair itches. I liked being blond."

"I hate it. Let's do it this way. I've got a list." Ariel opened a folded piece of paper, neatly printed. "We're either going to do this or not. If you want to be the star of *South Coast*."

"Okay, okay. Go ahead. Read your list."

"First, just to be safe, I had a tattoo made where my scar is. Do you think they can handle that when I'm you?"

"Show me."

"It's a little blue fish. With scales." Ariel pulled up her skirt. "How's that?"

"They won't like it much, but it's better than the scar. Scars they hate. Now I can hardly see it."

"You approve?"

Miranda shook her head. "I didn't say that, but I suppose I should get one too. Just to be safe. If I'm to be Tanya for the rest of the season, we need to be identical. For Josh. Who did it?"

"What?" Ariel was thinking about their altitude.

"The tattoo."

"I'll give you his card. He'll come to the house." Ariel cleared her throat, then plunked down her list on the table. "Okay, now don't get mad, Miranda. First question. What are my chances of getting a disease? A really serious disease?"

"I'll answer you straight. No guarantees. I've been in adult films for five years and all I've gotten is a little herpes. Genital herpes. It flares up once in a while. I take creams. They check me every month."

"How do they check you?"

"They draw blood. Next?"

"Okay. Delicate question. Suppose you go to Malta for me, and I go to Hawaii. What are your surprises? Josh and I have an open relation-ship. He sleeps around more than I do, but there are a few guys I see from time to time. For fun. How about you?"

"You're sure we're okay flying this plane straight out over the ocean?"

"I'm sure."

"I don't sleep with anyone regular. My boss shops me around. For money, okay. Very big money. Tax free. Paid in cash. There's one older man and one older woman. Both rich. I'm with them once or twice a month. I think of myself as their therapist. Sex therapist. They both have big names."

"You mean, I might know them?"

"The woman. You may have met her."

"Shit. I don't like sleeping with women."

"You've done it, right?"

"Once at Yale. My French...teacher. Shit, I can't believe I'm telling you this." Ariel checked her watch. "Sit back and finish your sherry. I've got to check the altitude. It's just a setting."

"We're not going to crash? I mean, *nobody* is flying this plane."

"We're not going to crash." Ariel rose from the table, trying not to rub against Miranda as she passed by.

"I hate sherry," said Miranda.

Ariel took her bearings. They were flying at 10,000 feet.

"KFRLM to tower. Could you give me my heading?"

"WNW with cross winds at 10,000 feet."

"That's right. Over."

When Ariel returned, Miranda was checking her makeup, thinking of Josh Perrin.

"Okay, we're set," said Ariel. "Just relax. Where was I?"

"Fucking your French teacher. A woman."

"Oh, yeah. Just where I wanted to be. Okay, let's get back to my list. Number Two. My big fear is screwing up on the set. On *South Coast* the hardest thing is staying awake. Boredom. You sit around waiting while they set the lighting and the sound. Then they mess around with make-up. What's the biggest problem with porno?"

"Adult entertainment. That's what they put on my IRS statement. Position is the problem. They stick you out there for ten minutes with your ass up in the air and your legs spread so wide you feel like Nebraska. It's either too hot or it's freezing cold, and all the time your male lead is trying to maintain an erection."

Miranda laughed and then Ariel laughed.

"I guess that is a problem," said Ariel.

"Droopy dicks. For position I do yoga. It keeps me limber. When you're on the set, you need to stretch between takes. Remember that. What's next?"

"What about orgasms?"

Miranda laughed. "It hardly ever happens. You fake it. They start and stop and oil you up. They change camera angles and the lights go up and down. Only the guy needs to come. They shoot that in all kinds of ways. The three angle come shot. Close, closer, and all over your face. Camera work is much more imaginative in porno."

"Adult entertainment."

"That too. Much more creative than it ever is on television. Study all the angles of *After the Prom*. I have a whole wall of my films at home. You watch them closeup. I mean it all depends on how much art Art wants to put into it. Art's my director. He shows me the script and I do the best I can. Some of it's just like modeling. The rest comes natural when you're a woman. Two things to remember. You're an actress, and you know how to fuck. What can go wrong?"

"Everything. I don't know any of your people. I watched *After the Prom* six times just to get an idea of what it's like. You say there's a script?"

"Of course there is. Donald writes most of them. He's a dwarf."

"Oh, really!" Ariel laughed that Yale laugh. "Is he in the films?"

"He was, several years ago, but he got hurt. Now he's a writer."

"And who's the guy who bangs you on the leather couch?"

"God. That's his stage name. He's the one I like to work with most."

"Who's Moe?"

"Moe's our comic dick. He's always hard. Mr. Fuzzy Wuzzy. He's real smart. He's a licensed broker. Buys real estate. He never enters me."

"What?"

"It's in the contract. Just oral sex. We use another guy for inside shots. Guaranteed clean. Inspected that day. Make your feel better?"

"A little. I'm terrified of sexual diseases."

"Okay. So?"

"Next question. Where do you shoot these films?"

"Stupendous Productions. The largest studio in Los Angeles. They shoot five films at a time, five days a week."

"You finish them up in one day?"

"What do you think we are, a cheap porno outfit? Some of them take two weeks."

"And who's they? The rest of the crew?"

"I told you about Art and Donald. Stupendous is Stu Eister. Mr.

Porno. I'm on his A-list. He has four types of films. The teenage whack jobs. That's where we all started. Stu tries the young girls out on kids whack-off films."

"Do I call him Stu?"

"Everyone calls him Stu."

"So, what else?"

"Let's see. There's the weirdo fetish stuff. I hate that group. They have their own building. One of them is always getting busted for something or other, but it's a real money-maker. Then there's lesbian films. I've done a few. Run by Flavia. Stu's wife. Very arty stuff. The sign on her office reads: *Check your cocks at the door*."

"A sense of humor."

"It's not like *South Coast*. Then there's the A-group. That's me. The best writers, cameramen, directors, and editors in the business. The Chinese government just sent some students over to see how we do it. They want to make adult films too."

Ariel laughed. "It sounds like fun."

"It's a good life. They treat me like a queen. We even go on location."

"Just like *South Coast*. Moe told me. Funny dick. Maybe we should get right down to it and exchange roles for the summer. Malta for French Frigate Cove."

"One step at a time. You do a week at my job, and I'll do a week at yours. Then we'll talk. Anything else?"

"How about love?"

"Love is not a word in my vocabulary, sis." Miranda's eyes grew hard. "Jon, I fuck sometimes. Just for fun. He gives me stock tips. He's in the next one. *Professor Max*. They'll send you the script. Anything else?"

"So *he* does enter you."

"Not on the set."

Ariel's watch beeped. "Okay, *sis*. Let's turn this plane around before we cross the International Dateline. I'll do a week at your job, and you do a week at mine. Agreed?"

"Agreed." Miranda followed her back to the cockpit.

"And have a good time with Josh."

- 2 -

Groves and Jones were seated in the *Flem* conference room facing Ruddy Drumrock and six lawyers. Slides of Josh Perrin and Ariel O'Brien flashed on the far wall to gasps and groans and cheers.

"When did you take these?" asked one of the lawyers.

"Last Saturday night, at Ariel O'Brien's place on the ocean."

"You have it on digital?" asked another attorney. "Like a film?"

"Exactly," said Jones. "Thousands of possible stills."

"Still," said Drumrock, "this is not really scandal. They live together off and on, isn't that true?"

"They're..." said Groves. "You know, we've been on this project..."

Drumrock rose to his full height of five foot five, and shushed them. "Yes, yes. It's very fine work. I was just making a point. A fine point. For once we have something the public wants that is *not* scandal. It's wholesome fucking, see what I mean?"

Groves cleared his throat.

The boss continued, "What *Flem* has here is something very special. Two people fucking who love one another. Imagine if we had this with George and Martha Washington, or Grover Cleveland and his young bride."

"Cleveland had a young bride?"

"She was twenty-one when he married her. Imagine if we had that?"

No one said a word.

"Sam, what do you think?" asked Drumrock.

"Well...my first question is simply this. *Is it them?* It looks like Josh Perrin and Ariel O'Brien, but is it really them? When we vet this, we have to be sure. You shot it at Ariel O'Brien's house, you say. Where exactly is that?"

"Point Dume," said Groves. "The Point Dume Club."

Mr. I. stroked his chin. "I thought you boys could never get in there."

"We tried before, but this time they let us in."

"We followed them from the Dublin Club," said Jones. "Perrin left his car there. He was too drunk or loaded. She drove that fucking pick--up truck of hers. And they let us in behind them."

Sam was skeptical. "Don't you think that was strange?"

"What the hell does it matter how they got in" asked Drumrock. "They got in. You can see it's them engaged in intercourse. That's obvious. We can't show all of it. We're not Larry Flynt. But we can show Josh Perrin with half of Miss O'Brien's breast in his mouth. His face and her face, as clear as day."

"It was night," said Jones. "Just to be factual. For the lawyers."

"Can you run the whole thing as a tape?" asked one lawyer. "I mean, like a film?"

Groves made a few adjustment, and ran it for the troops. They were pleased. They were very pleased. The lawyers were pleased.

Drumrock had one concern. "Her hair is very black. Blacker than the other shots we've run of her. Explain that, Bud."

"She had her hair done the day before," said Jones. "Her real hair color is dark brown. From her high school yearbook pictures. When she was Senior Prom Queen. We can assume if she drove *her* truck, and they had sex at *her* address, it must be them."

No one spoke. Drumrock sat down and poured himself a glass of water. "I'm asking you guys. Our legal defense team. Doesn't that make sense?"

"Yes," said Sam. "It was them. It had to be them. But I still don't see the angle of the story. It's not a scandal. They just had sex."

"Who buys our weekly, gentlemen?"

"WOMEN." They all said it together.

"That's right. And why do men not buy *Flem*? They're embarrassed. They think it's a gossip sheet for women. If they do buy it, they have to hide it from their wives, like *Playboy*. But if we have photographs of their favorite female fantasy, and she's shown with the major male heartthrob of the age, a guy buying vodka at a liquor store would be just as inclined to buy *Flem* as his wife. And why?" Drumrock was now standing. "Anyone?"

No one said anything.

"Well, I'll tell you why. Because this is clean and wholesome FUCK-ING. I never use that word, but here it applies. There's no scandal. Our all-American male can take it home to his wife or girlfriend, and wrap it around a bouquet of roses! That's the kind of fun we can have with this. At their expense, of course. We can't show his...organ. And we can't show him...entering her. But we can show his mouth upon her pale white breast, and we can show her eyes rolling back into her head as she..."

"Comes," they all said.

"Experiences orgasm. That's what every American wants. Isn't it Sam?"

Sam nodded. "I'll vet that."

"Josh Perrin and Ariel O'Brien in bed together, like two Greek gods. It's a five million seller. Maybe more. And everyone will be happy about it."

"Even them," said Groves. "Just in time to negotiate next year's contract!"

SEVEN

"Let's stay in touch by cell phone just to be safe," said Miranda. "Your first day there is gonna be an eye-opener. I'll help you through it step by step."

Ariel was in the Jag, halfway to Thousand Oaks. "I'm at the gate. This place is huge."

"*Stupendous.* I told you. The MGM, Dreamworks, and Disney of Adult Entertainment all rolled into one. Gonna blow your mind."

Ariel kept fixing her hair. Patting it down. "What do I do to get inside?"

"Just wave. They know the car. Blow Hal a kiss. He's the old guy. Worked on *Deep Throat* when he was a kid. He has AIDS. We keep him around to remind us. Blow him a kiss. Then follow the map."

"Hi, Hal." Ariel pursed her lips.

"Hi, beautiful. Say hello to Stu for me."

"Sure will, Hal." Ariel made a mental note about *gonna*. She and Miranda would have to talk. Josh would spot her *gonnas* in a second. "Miranda..."

"Listen, I'm off to makeup. Park in front under the green waterfall. Nancy called. I'll handle it." She clicked off.

Ariel looked around for her parking space. They were labeled: Hairy Moe. Dildo Don. God Rod. Mira Mirror. That had to be it. She pulled in and turned off the engine.

It was so nice to drive her own car at nine in the morning dressed for the day, instead of crawling into a limo at 5:00 a.m. in sweats and sneak-ers clutching a cold cup of bad instant coffee. She reached for her map, but before she could study it, the blond guy fucking Miranda in *After the Prom* grabbed her by the arm, then kissed her on the neck.

"So, you ready for Hawaii?" he asked.

"Call him God," Mira had said. "He hates Gotthold and Gott sounds too German."

"Sure, God," said Ariel. "I am, and you're not going. A little vacation after *Professor Max*." She held up her script.

"It's all movement. Panofsky's Theory of Dynamism? Which way are you going? Flavia's Palace?"

Ariel looked back at the green waterfall. "What? Did you say Panof-sky?" She hadn't heard that name since Yale.

"You forget, I studied philosophy. Heidelberg."

Ariel laughed. She stuck the map in her jeans and let God lead her where he might.

"Know the Dublin Club?" he asked.

She tried to think what to say. "Heard about it."

"We might do a shoot there. There's a restaurant scene in the next one." He held up his script. *Professor Max*. "Stu likes it."

"What?"

"The Dublin Club. You better get your rub down. I'll see you in a bit."

They entered a large building that smelled of bath oil.

"Mira, are you drunk?" God asked. "To the left."

"I am a little. Too much *blanc d 'blanc*." Ariel followed the scent of bath oil through a door marked **Massage**. Her rub down. What did Mir-anda say her name was? Margaret. The tall Swede who spoke seven lan-guages.

- 2 -

"Mira, they want you pale today. Donald's obsession. *Professor Max*. The body is a painter's most basic canvas."

"Who said that? Panofsky?"

Margaret laughed. "Stu, of course. Or are you hung over?" She began to strip away Ariel's clothing. First the boots, then the blouse, and finally the jeans. When Margaret reached for the panties, Ariel pushed her back and pulled them off herself. Margaret examined them, then dropped them into a plastic bag. "Stu likes red."

"I'm sorry," Ariel replied, placing her cell phone on a chair.

"You are sleepy today. Red. Red panties. Never white. White is Flavia's color. These are for *men*. Mira Monroe is for men. Or have you forgotten?" Margaret held up the plastic bag. "You know, Mira. One thousand dollars! For the collectors. Earth to Mira. You must be returning from a lost weekend."

Ariel nodded. "Red panties. What was I thinking?" Panofsky and his theory of dynamism had thrown her off balance. The cast of *South Coast* had never heard of Erwin Panofsky.

"Okay. Up on the table."

Ariel climbed onto the cold steel massage table and waited. Margaret was looking at her funny.

"Now what?" Ariel asked.

"Now what? What's this? Open up."

Ariel parted her thighs. She was a bit uneasy with this tall blonde whose hair was lighter than hers. Lighter than Mira Monroe's. And natural.

"This fishy thing?" said Margaret.

"Oh, that. That's a tattoo. I got it over the weekend. A night on the town with..."

"Okay, okay. Stu will have a squid. *No body piercings and no tattoos.* Who do you think you are, a biker chick? On your belly. Mira Monroe is no biker chick."

As Margaret spread oil on her back, Ariel glanced at the clock. 9:30.

"Okay, deep breaths." Margaret grabbed her left leg and pulled it sideways.

Ariel was beginning to wonder what Miranda was up to on the set of *South Coast*. The massage made her sleepy.

"Your muscles are tight. I'll soften them up till you feel like a lump of pounded dough."

After thirty minutes of deep massage, Mira fell asleep, to be wakened ten minutes later by the makeup man, Pan.

"Donald wants you pale, sweetheart," he said. "First we have to paint the fuzz. Gold. Roll over. Let's see. Oh my god."

"What?"

"What have you been up to? A little blue tattoo. On the basic canvas of the body. Stu will have a squid."

With a spray can, he began to paint her pubic hair with gold paint. "Cold?"

"Very. Leave me a little room to pee."

Pan laughed. "Now white. All over. Just a cream. From head to foot. Donald wants you looking like a cadaver. Or a ghost. No lighting tricks today. Not for restoration. *Professor Max.* Hold still. This stuff has to go on evenly. It smears and then you can't wash it off!"

Ariel sat up. She was now a blonde with gold pubic hair, and a body painted white as chalk. "How long will it take for this *paint* to wear off?"

"A day or two, Mira dear. Now a little touchup on the upstairs hair." He took up his pallet and applied some paint. Real paint!

"Well?" a buzzer sounded.

"Ready," was all Pan said.

With hardly a beat, Ariel was whisked away on an electric cart with only a towel wrapped around her white body. Names went whirling through her brain. Moe, the comic dick with whom she'd spoken on the phone. Donald, the dwarf who wrote the scripts. Art Hotz, the director. And then all her female co-stars: Cinder and Angel and Gasquet. There was also Stu Eister and God and Panofsky.

It did get her blood boiling. It was sooooooo not like *South Coast.* Not boring. For Ariel, it was a real challenge. She was an actress playing an actress playing an actress. Keeping that straight could never be boring!

Halfway down the hallway of Studio A, her cell phone rang.

"Hey, we're on location in Brentwood," said Miranda. "Where are you?"

"Somewhere in Studio A. I'm wrapped in a towel and painted white. Don't ask."

Miranda was chuckling. "That's Donald's stuff. He writes it, but it all comes from Stu. His UC Restoration Theatre days. He owns the largest collection of Restoration costumes in the world."

"How nice for him."

"And a theatre in Victoria to go with it. Remember just one thing."

"What?"

"Keep stretching. How's Margaret?"

"Fascinating. I know I've seen her around somewhere."

"Could be. Well, I'm up. Josh and me. He can't keep his hands off my ass."

"How nice for you. How about Anaca?"

"She's in a bad mood and Bruce is sick. He's here, but he has the flu. I'll probably get it. Remember what I told you about being on the set." "Just keep stretching. I'm out here in a towel, riding around on a golf cart. And a warning. The name John Dryden. Never say it! *Never! NEV-ER!* Unless you want to be unemployed. Remember, you are me and I don't want to lose my day job. Bye."

Ariel shook her head as Miranda clicked off. Her cart sped through a doorway onto the set.

"It's the way he remembers it, Art."

"Backstage?"

"Yeah. The dressing rooms. Let's try the lighting levels again. Darker. Hey, Harlow."

Ariel didn't miss a beat. "Good morning, Art."

She caught her breath and looked around. The costumes were racked out on the set. "Oh, yes," she recalled. "The first shot begins backstage in the dressing room."

"I think it was Sedley. Should we ask Stu? What do you think, Jake?"

Ariel had it. Donald was the dwarf. He smiled. Moe was the hairy one. He gave her a hug. Art was the director. Jake was the camera man. He was looking at Art. Then there was Cinder, the little redhead, and Gasquet, the tall and voluptuous brunette. All three women were in towels.

"Where the hell is God?" asked Art.

"God is getting a shave," said Donald, sitting at his writing desk. "Do we have the Rhinegraves?"

"The what?"

"The divided skirt for Nell?"

Art Hotz ignored Donald's question. "Okay, actors. Let me see my cast. Moe. Professor Max."

Moe stood up. He was dressed in a late Sixties three piece suit

"Sit down, Moe. Mira, our Nell Gwynn. You'll need your wig. Where the hell is God, our good King Charles?"

Gotthold Roddick rushed in holding up an elaborate wig. "Here. Sorry."

"Cinder as Mrs. Barry."

Cinder stood up in her towel and bowed. "I'm freezing, Art."

"Wardrobe mistress, robes!" Art roared.

A fat little woman in black appeared. Candice, thought Ariel. Or Candy. That was her name.

"And Moll. Moll the dresser. Angel?"

Angel. That was the one to look for, the new girl. Stu's mistress. Dark eyes, dark makeup, a *chola* from the barrio. Maybe nineteen. She jumped from the teen whack-off films to the A-list in two months.

Angel received her terry cloth robe first, and then the others slipped theirs on. It was freezing on the set. Too much air conditioning.

"Stu likes it that way," Miranda had said.

"Okay?" Art Hotz sat at the head of the work table, thumbing the script. "Coffee?"

A young man looming in the darkness moved toward the table, pushing a metal cart. He poured Ariel a cup, asking. "Cream?"

"Uh, no." Ariel tried to remember which was right. Cream or no cream?

"Okay, let's get started," said Art. "*Professor Max*, redux. First shot. We're in the dressing room of the Jung Theatre. Moll is dressing the two actresses. Mrs. Gwynn and Mrs. Barry. Now, get this right. You are *not* Nell Gwynn and Mrs. Barry. You are two college girls playing actresses. From Stu's dream life. Right, Donald?"

"Exactly," said the little man seated at his writing table.

"Both of you stand there naked, in all your very white powder. Angel applies it in tiny dabs. Then you begin the process of dressing. You are *not* reading lines from the play. Got it?"

"Which play would that be?" asked Angel.

"Which play? Donald?"

"The play was *Secret Love*," said Donald. "By guess who?"

"Don't say it." They mouthed it: *Dryden*.

Donald continued. "Mira, you play Florimell."

Ariel had to pinch herself. Florimell? This was a fuck film. She was ready to get reamed up to her elbows by God himself, while the writer and director were talking of wigs and powder. And Ariel knew the play. She *almost* said, "It was titled *The Maiden Queen* when I did it at Yale." But she strangled her thoughts with a cough.

"Okay, actors. Up on your feet. Let's set the lights. Look for your marks. Angel, a whiff of powder at first. Cinder, you're looking on."

"I'm fucking freezing in here, Art. Look how hard my nipples are!"

"That's good, that's good. That's what Stu wants. Hard nipples. Now lights. Okay, Jake. Let's see what we get here. Angel. More powder on Mira's muff. Bend down and give us a back door shot. Now come back up slowly. Try to pull the shift on over your head. Angel, yank it up as you apply the powder. Okay, pull down the shift and hand her the wig. I need your ass up higher, Mira. And Angel, when you put that powder on her muff, I want your nose almost in it. Can you get that Jake?"

"Let's run it one more time and slow it down, Art."

"Crank out a two shot," said the director. "Bring in the closeup cam."

"Angel?"

"Huh?" Angel looked lost.

"Angel, pull her shift off."

"Her what?"

"That funny slip. It's called a shift. Knees wider, Mira. I want to see glowing cunt. Pan, oil her up!"

Ariel giggled, bending naked before the camera with her legs spread.

"Moe, move slowly through the door. Got it?"

"Got it."

"Let's try it with the lines. Mira."

"Okay. 'He kissed me in the library. When I was working at the desk.' "

"Bend more to me, Mira."

Ariel felt a twinge across her neck.

"Move in, Jake."

It was twenty minutes before Gotthold Roddick began licking on her clit. Ariel's legs were straight up in the air and her back aching. Miranda was right. What was on her mind at that moment had nothing to do with sex. Ariel wanted a warm bath, a muscle relaxant, and a nap.

When God entered her all oiled up, Ariel sneezed.

The whole set burst out laughing.

"Shit, Mira keep your legs up, and what the hell's so funny?"

"Moe is making faces."

"Okay, let's cut," said Hotz. "God, we'll try the diamond scene. On the bed. Let's get the lights set up. Hang it between her tits as though it was on fire. And don't drop it. It belongs to Stu."

"It belongs to me," said Angel.

"I thought I had my clothes on for that shot?" said God.

"We'll shoot it with just your wig. Put it over Lincoln."

God covered his penis with the long blond periwig, then stood by the bed where Mira Monroe reclined.

"You want me to hang the diamond on it?" Moe laughed.

"Right on old Abe. She pulls off the wig, and there's the diamond."

"It's hard to keep it hard with all this comedy," Gotthold complained.

"This is Stu's wet dream. It's not for Disney. How are you, Moe?"

"Hard."

"Moe is always hard," said Angel. "He's a method actor."

And that was the way the day went when Miranda called Ariel late.

- 3 -

Eyes closed, Ariel reached for the phone.

"I've been trying to reach you for hours."

"I took a seconal. What time is it?"

"Two a.m. I can't sleep. I'm so bored. How was your first day?"

"You woke me from a drug-induced sleep."

"So tell me. Was it what you thought it would be?"

Ariel sat up on the pillow. Miranda's pillow. "It was interesting. My back is out, and I hurt inside from Gottholt Roddick's twenty inch dick. And there's a rash around my new tattoo. But aside from that I pulled it off. Is that really his last name? Rod dick?" She laughed.

"Really. He has a Ph.D. in philosophy, but that's not why the world will remember him. Keep doing your stretching. There's a Jaccuzzi on the roof. I'd use it if I were you. Did you meet Stu yet?"

"Not yet. How was it on the set of *South Coast*?"

"Boring. Bruce has the flu and he came to work anyway, so we'll all get it, I suppose."

"You told me that." Ariel rolled over on her back until it hurt. "Are you at Josh's house?"

"No. I'm at Ariel O'Brien's house and I hate her underwear. All white."

"I know, I know. I got yelled at when I wore them to work today."

"Red or black. Shows some residue. Well, gotta go sis. Gonna get up at five again."

" 'Got to' and 'going to.' I never say 'gotta' and I never say 'gonna' unless they're in the script that way. Yale took away my slang."

"Poor you. Well, I've got to go. Enjoy the jacuzzi. Oh, and there's that lady I see once a month. I'll call you about her tomorrow. She likes clothes pins on her nipples."

"Let's talk tomorrow. Probably a good thing if we're not seen together for a while. You know. Groves and Jones."

"Groves and Jones. Just so. Night." Miranda hung up the phone, took a sip of water from the bathroom tap, then crawled back into Ariel O'Brien's bed, careful not to wake Josh.

He wanted to show her that tape again, *Fashion Sluts*. He said he had a lead on the girl, Mira Monroe.

EIGHT

It was one in the morning on a Wednesday night. The offices on Wilshire Boulevard were empty except for the cleaning staff. Bud Jones was thumbing through next week's *Flem*, laughing and joking with Groves.

"A ten page spread, Ray. Ten pages. It'll make us famous, if it don't make us rich."

"It'll make us rich too," said Groves.

"We just get a bonus."

"I held back forty minutes of the two of them laughing and smoking and fucking away, and I showed it to an interested professional."

"Who would that be?"

"Stu Eister of Stupendous Productions. He wants to sell it on the internet. Under an assumed name. It will make us all a fortune."

Bud Jones put down the stack of tabloids. "You mean Stu and me and you. But what about the lawyers?"

"If it's on the internet, it's out there. When they sue, Josh and Ariel get half. It'll be millions after this article hits. They can't stop it on the internet. It's just out there. So why not cash in on it? They'll be the hottest couple in America by Friday."

"How do you know their lawyers will want to deal?"

"Bud, in this town that's all lawyers do. You know the sound is bad. What did Mr Porno think about that?"

"Stu will get two of his 'actors' to dub in the groans. His very adult actors. And Stu knows how to deal with lawyers."

- 2 -

At six a.m. on Friday, Miranda was grumpy in the limo. It was to be her last day on the set of *South Coast* before their summer shoot. Before Malta. Josh would be in Los Angeles making a movie while Mira Monroe was off on some island with the most boring people in the world.

"You're having cream with your coffee," Josh remarked. "You only have cream when you're hung over."

"I haven't had any sleep. That's the same thing. And you can't call this coffee."

"I don't know, Air. You're just not yourself these days. You're so up-tight and you can't sleep worth a damn."

"I'm gonna miss you, Josh."

"And 'gonna.' Where did that come from? Are you returning to your childhood days? Before Yale? Well, I have a surprise for you. A real surprise. A double surprise."

"Tonight?"

"Tomorrow. When all this stuff is over." He gave her a warm kiss on the neck as Miranda balanced the hot coffee on her knee.

"So what is it? We're getting engaged?"

"Don't joke. You hate marriage more than I do. Let's have fun today. Kiss Anaca again and mean it. Fuck up your lines ten takes in a row till Larry has a stroke. Then we'll go have some fun. An old friend of mine is doing me a favor."

"An old girlfriend?"

"She's old all right, but she's not a girlfriend. She likes women. Let's leave it a secret. Something to look forward to on an otherwise boring day."

- 3 -

"I need a touch up on the forelocks, Tanya."

"What am I, Olivia? A horse?"

"You are to Larry, Miss O'Brien. Top pedigree. A front runner. You carry the show."

Miranda said nothing. She was thumbing the last two pages of her script when Larry shouted, "This is where you run, Air. Let's walk it through first. With the lines."

Miranda looked around then walked/jogged down the roadway. "Now that I lost my brother, this is where I turn?"

"By the car. Just behind it as you watch him drive off. Then you run along behind." Larry was out there without his hat. His hair was that sick, faded yellow old men get when their skin goes gray and their eyes start to dim. He looked old and tired.

"How fast?"

"How fast can you run?"

They were high up Mulholland Highway, looking down toward the Beverly Hills Hotel where a luncheon was waiting for all, cast and crew. But the crew was anxious to finish, and the cast members were all sick or stoned or just plain tired of the whole thing. Only Miranda felt sadness. She had been with *South Coast* for a week and a half, and though they were the most boring group of people she had ever worked with, she knew she would soon lose Josh.

"Okay?" she asked.

"You turn to the left as he drives off, and then you run out until he misses the turn and goes over the cliff. Then you stop. Stop at the Oombu tree."

"The which?"

"The one with the big roots. Then turn and give me your lines, and we fade out for the whole *fucking* season. Hear that cast?"

The cast and crew cheered.

Josh got into the car and slammed the door. Then he got out and a stunt driver drove off furiously. Miranda ran off down the road after the black Mustang while a camera truck followed close behind. As the Mustang shot round the curve, Miranda looked back and said her line: "Now that I lost my brother...I think I'll leave too."

"That's fine," said Larry. "We're finished. End of season. Let's go celebrate. A table is waiting at the Beverly Hills Hotel. In the garden."

It was a little after noon on a warm sunny day on the first of May. They drove off together in a long caravan of motor homes and limos and equipment trucks. Like a circus, Miranda thought.

- 4 -

When they arrived, Anaca had slipped into a red satin dress and Josh put on his jodhpurs. Bruce wore a top hat. Holly draped a cape over her slender shoulders. Olivia stole the show in a one piece bathing suit and sandals.

The famous cast was now assembled, seated in the garden of the most beautiful hotel in the world according to Dave Ivy, who sat at the head of the table. Miranda in a filmy pink mini-dress was at his right hand, and Josh Perrin at his left. Ariel and Josh, the princess and prince of *South Coast*. That's what Dave Ivy thought. That's what the cast and crew thought. That's what the whole world thought, except for Miranda.

As two waiters brought them champagne, Dave Ivy stood up and raised his glass. "To our *fifth* successful season, and still high up in the ratings. And to my wonderful stars."

Dave took the hands of Josh and Miranda, as Anaca cringed.

"*This* is what makes it wonderful for me every day," said Dave, "working with Josh and Ariel and Holly and Thor and Jenny and Bruce, my son. With all of you. I know you are getting a little old for high school, but let's look at the other side of it. You are the owners of horses and boats and planes and ranches, a French restaurant, and a nudist camp. Right, Anaca? You have homes in Malibu and the Hollywood Hills and the south of France. Josh has a garage full of sports cars and all of your parents are rich. You started here as kids and look where you are now! And I'm not too bad off myself. Life has been good to all of us on *South Coast*. And you all have given me back a small part of my youth, my own high school days. For that, I thank you."

They all applauded.

"So let's drink to the bottom line. Just two more years and we're into reruns. Then we can all retire."

"Two more weeks and we'll be in Malta," yelled Holly. "Except for Josh. Poor Josh."

"Poor me." Josh was holding Miranda's hand, thinking how much in love he was with Ariel.

"I want to throw up," yelled Anaca.

She rushed off to the ladies room. When she returned, she held the latest copy of *Flem*. On the front page was a revealing photo of Ariel O'Brien and Josh Perrin. She held it up so all could see, then plunked it down over Ariel's purse:

JOSH & ARIEL: HOW HOT DOES IT GET?
10 SIZZLING PAGES OF PHOTOS AND QUOTES

Miranda looked down at the picture. She flipped the tabloid open to the center section and stared in disbelief. There was a blowup of Josh Perrin sucking Ariel O'Brien's left breast right down into his throat. Or at least, she thought it was Ariel's.

"Ten pages," was all she could say.

Josh stared across the table, his face bright red. He looked at Miranda but she said nothing. She was studying the photograph. Josh was Josh all right, but who was the girl? Ariel or Miranda? The painting above them was the one in Ariel's bedroom at Point Dume. The John Piper.

Anaca stood behind them, watching the whole thing up close. She looked for the tiny flecks Ariel had in her left eye, the ones that lit up when she was angry, but they were not there.

"How the hell...?" Josh sighed. "It must have been the night we drove from the Dublin Club. See, there's your bandage." Josh shook his head.

TEN PAGES OF BLISS spouted the blurb in flaming red ink.

Dave Ivy stood up again, over his Shrimp Louis, and smiled. "Josh, Josh, Josh. So what? The two of you are in love. Everyone knows that. Right, Anaca?"

Anaca caught her breath.

Dave held high the center section, thrusting it forward for the cast and crew. "This is what love looks like, right? *This* is beautiful." He flipped over to a full color photo of Josh Perrin with his head between Miranda's legs, her eyes floating back in her head in ecstasy.

Miranda saw the bandage. Josh was right. It was her, not Ariel. It was really Mira Monroe and to *her* it was all very funny. She'd done this stuff thousands of times as a blonde. Not as Tanya of *South Coast*, of course, and not as a ten-page spread in *Flem*, but what the hell? What had she been working for all these years if not to be seen? This was America, she smiled. This was fucking America!

"So you think--" Josh began.

Dave Ivy stopped him. "I know what you're thinking, all of you. Sponsors will cancel. You're wrong. Who are our sponsors? Ladies' perfumes--and men's colognes and cars and beer and *Viagra*." He gave a great cheer.

The waiters all stopped what they were doing.

"*This*," Dave held up the centerfold, "will boost their sales a thousand times over. *Men* will bring this *fucking Flem* home to their wives because this is beauty. Look." He pointed at Miranda's left breast. "This is fucking Aphrodite. This is the love of the Greek gods. Just look at Ariel's...thighs."

Miranda laughed. "They really show everything," was all she could say.

But Dave Ivy was on a roll as he continued, "Tomorrow you two will be on the front page of every newspaper in the country. And on every network news show. I'm proud of you. You couldn't have done a better job of publicity if you'd arranged this whole thing yourselves. I'm proud of you. And I'm glad you never got that boob job, Ariel. They look so *fucking* perfect, just the way God made them."

He extended the twenty inch foldout of Miranda's left breast with Josh Perrin's mouth all over it. Everyone cheered, even the waiters.

"Hurray for love," yelled Bruce.

Nearby at a Hollywood bar, Groves and Jones were also celebrating.

"We just launched ourselves into the stratosphere," said Bud Jones. "I got a lawyer who'll handle O'Brien and Perrin. You can order your Porsche now!"

He was roaring the raucous laughter only great wealth can bring to little people.

To Ariel O'Brien, the results of the day were even more delightful.

"Where are you now, my dear Miranda?"

"At the hotel. In the ladies' room. What do I do now?"

"Exactly what you *are* doing. As me. Groves and Jones got you as me, and boy do we have them. All I have to do is be you."

"Speaking of which, you have an appointment tomorrow. In Bel Air. I told you about my once a month."

"Appointment?" asked Ariel.

"Listen, I'm in a rush. Call you later?"

Ariel continued to laugh. "Hang on for a sec. It's so funny, sis. You don't know what we're sitting on. *Flem* has my name and your face."

"They have a lot more than that. They have my clitoris, if you look closely."

"*Yes* and they have it *all wrong*. Just smile for the press when you leave. You and Josh. And smile for me too. You know what to say?"

"Not really. I've never dealt with the press before."

"Just say you're in love and love is private And don't look hurt. That's the secret. Enjoy it. Give Josh a kiss on the cheek and smile. Everyone will be on your side. We have to talk."

"Yeah, you're damned right." Miranda clicked off and stormed out of the ladies' room. *I'm going back to finish my dessert*, she thought.

When she returned to her seat, Dave Ivy had a surprise for her.

"Look who's joined us," said Dave. "Your friend Bonnie, back from Broadway. Her run is over. Don't worry, Anaca. She's not coming back. Right, kid?"

"Right. So...how nice. My old best friend."

Miranda gasped, then gave Bonnie a hug. So much was happening.

"Okay, troupe" said Dave. "Ready for your farewell photos? Our waiter warns me the press is swarming out there. Smile and wave. What a great way to end the season."

"There's always Malta," yelled Holly, the youngest of the cast. Her breasts had recently been done and she wanted to show them off.

- 5 -

The first time Ariel met Stu Eister, he was listening to Gotthold Roddick. They were deep in conversation about food.

"It didn't make me sick," said the older man. "It was an interesting taste."

"That's the point," said God. "There is food that is good, and you swallow it and it pleases you. It goes down and you smack your lips. And there is food that's bad, and you either don't eat it at all, or it makes you sick. But food that is interesting is not either good or bad. That pasta I served you was lacking a real sauce, so I came up with a little tomato soup and some Italian salad mix."

"So that's what that taste was. It stayed with me all night, but you are correct. It was interesting. It did not come back up, and yet I could say it did not quite stay down."

God was laughing so hard, tears were in his eyes. "You mean it stayed there in your stomach as a gas?"

Stu was laughing too, in a strange way. Ariel had heard that laugh before, but she couldn't remember where. "I guess that's what your dinner was," said Stu. "A gas."

"That's my point," said God, still laughing. "The reason why everyone keeps asking for *Professor Max* is because he goes back and forth between the three women. His wife, the freshman, and the graduate student. And he keeps putting them off, even with an erection. Even with the sexy freshman--"

"Me," said Ariel, sidling up to the boss.

"Yes you, Mira, my dear," Stu tapped her hard on her left nipple. "He delays and delays and delays. The viewer has to wait for his gratification so it's not just another fuck film. There's tension! Is that your point, Gotthold?"

"Exactly. It's comedy. It's restored comedy. The viewer has to wait for the cum shots!"

"Certainly, it's Restoration comedy," said Stu, as he gave that sinister smirk Mira had warned about. "You'll have to come visit him sometime, Mira. The real Professor Max. He belongs to me, body and soul. Know what I mean?"

"You mean, you have him stuffed?" said Ariel. The way Stu Eister spoke the word 'belongs' gave Ariel a chill. "Would I enjoy his company?

The real Professor Max?"

Stu smiled. "God has seen him. Haven't you, God?"

Gotthold nodded, and his eyes went totally dead. "The real Professor Max is not stuffed, but he's been erased."

NINE

In front of the Beverly Hills Hotel, Josh and Miranda took a long time to say good-bye.

"You need to stay with me tonight, Air," Josh suggested. "The loonies will be out there looking for you."

Miranda thought it over. She wasn't Air. Besides, Bonnie was hanging around with old-time stories of their starvation days in Hollywood, and Miranda hardly knew who Bonnie was. Then there was Amanda Walters, the Bel Air lesbian with whom she had a one o'clock appointment.

"I don't think so, Josh. My cell phone has sixty-two messages."

"Come on. What did David say about *our* love?"

Miranda didn't want to think about it. "No." She pouted the way Ariel pouted on *South Coast*. "Tonight I want to be by myself."

"Okay." He kissed her on both eyes, then walked slowly down the drive. "I'll call you later."

Tonight Miranda wanted to be Miranda O'Neill. Not Mira Monroe or Tayna or Ariel, just herself. She looked at her ringing cell phone and gave off a howl. "This goddamn piece of Pavlovian shit is the only thing here that belongs to *me*. I can't even sleep in my own fucking bed."

"Car?" asked the valet.

Avoiding Bonnie, Miranda made for the company limo and was driven straight to her door.

Meanwhile, Ariel was on *her* cell phone answering as Ariel.

"Could you be in New York on Monday for *Morning World*?" asked the show's rep. "We'll fly you by private jet, and you can stay anywhere you like in Manhatten." He suggested several five star hotels.

"I don't think so," said Ariel. "Would you talk to Josh instead?"

"Yes."

These people you can't fuck with, her PR firm had told her.

Ariel was in Miranda's Jag, driving toward Santa Monica, answering as Ariel O'Brien.

Next, Nancy called and asked what to do.

"Nothing," said Ariel. "Take your vacation. The season is over."

"I know, but I've heard from everyone but the Pope. Your mother called."

"Go to Mexico. See your family."

"Air, are you serious?"

"David thinks it's the best publicity in the world. Go to Mexico and fuck a sailor. It will do you good."

"You sure?"

"I'm sure."

Nancy clicked off.

Next came a call from *Entertainment Hollywood*. "Is it true you're four months pregnant?"

Ariel laughed. "Not as far as I know. You guys should get up off your fat asses and do some real work. Investigate. You never get anything right."

Entertainment Hollywood hated her, anyway. They were the one program she was allowed to dump on.

By the time Ariel reached Miranda's garage, her agent was calling to say she'd received three big scripts. "Two are perfect, and they're willing to offer you millions."

Ariel had heard that before. When she got in the door, she flung off her shoes, unhitched her bra, and fell on the couch. She punched on the TV and there it was. Scenes from *South Coast* intercut with photos from *Flem*. Photos of Miranda, not Ariel, rolling her eyes back up into her head, in total ecstasy as Josh Perrin licked her ears.

"God," Ariel thought. "I have to call Miranda. She's probably going crazy. I have to ask her about that woman in Bel Air."

And then Miranda's phone rang. Ariel answered it. The voice on the other end was Amanda Walters, the woman who lived at the very top of Bel Air.

"Mira, dear, could you please pick up some spearmint leaves on your way?"

The tone was intimate. In the background, Ariel could hear that singer Josh was crazy about. Libby Holman, the one who had killed her husband. Or had he shot himself over her delicious infidelities?

"Where's the best place to find them?" Ariel asked. "I'm in a hurry."

"How would I know? Avoid the big drugstores. Try an upscale candy shop. They have the best spearmint leaves. The kind that make my tongue swell. Buy a pound. See you at one, honey bun. "

Ariel looked up her name in Miranda's phone book. Amanda Walters. Roscomere Drive.

Miranda called. Ariel picked up.

"She was married once," Miranda told her. "But she uses her maiden name. You can't miss the place. It's at the top of the hill. It's the biggest house in Bel Air. Security is better than the White House."

"How old is she?"

"Sixty."

Ariel took a seconal and fell into a deep sleep.

Miranda, on the other hand, could not sleep at all.

Josh called her at two a.m. "How are you holding up?"

"I'm okay. I turned off the TV."

"Good. That's the way to handle it. Meet me at the Malibu Inn for lunch. Oneish. Take a cab, so they can't follow you. I have a surprise."

"Jeez, Josh. I don't know if I can stand any more surprises. And where's Bonnie?"

"She's asleep. Right next to me. See you tomorrow."

- 2 -

After searching a large Bi Rite to no avail, Ariel finally located her pound of spearmint leaves at Candy World in Westwood.

"What the hell has happened to spearmint leaves?" Ariel asked the sales girl. "I can't find them anywhere. Only here, where they're four dollars a pound. Why is that?"

"Don't ask me, dear. I just work here. Eight dollars an hour. I'm quitting next week. I guess the owners stock what people can't find in the grocery stores. We sell lots of these." She weighed them, wrapped the green sugared leaves in gold paper, spinning the bundle into a tight packet, tying them with a silver twist wire. "Maybe spearmint leaves are highly addictive. Most of the people who buy them look like addicts." She laughed. "Not you, of course."

"No, not me."

Ariel revved up the Jag, which she was beginning to like, then drove up Hilgard to Sunset, crossing into Bel Air through the West Gate. The whole place looked like it was private. There should have been a sign, she thought. POOR PEOPLE KEEP OUT UNLESS YOU'RE MAIDS AND GARDENERS. That was the impression the neighborhood gave off. All roads north of UCLA *looked* private.

The house of Amanda Walters was at the top of Stoner Canyon. The name always amused Ariel, given the nature of the inhabitants and their children. The same brats as portrayed on *South Coast.*

Why am I so goddamn mad at the rich? she thought. *I'm rich myself.*

Maybe in Miranda's skin, a porno star, she felt more vulnerable. Like all her wealth could be taken away in a day.

At the guard house, two men in suits briefly examined the back seat of her car. One of them smirked, then motioned the Jag inside the high walls of the estate.

There's rich and there's super-rich, Ariel thought.

At the house, she was met by a woman in a tailored dress who turned out to be Amanda Walters's secretary, a dumpy blonde in blue silk shoes with a pink and white face. "You're late. Did you get her the candy?"

Ariel held up the little gold packet.

"Well?" said the dumpy blonde. "You know what she wants. Something to suck on."

Ariel made for the front door.

"What is the matter with you today, Miss Monroe? Back door!

Around to the right for the help! Dolores is pouring your milk bath. Today she's chilling half-and-half. A little more cream in the mix."

The dumpy blonde dragged her around to the side of the house, and opened the kitchen door. Ariel was not quite sure what she should do. As the dumpy blonde eyed her, Ariel sat at the kitchen table, waiting for instructions. If only Miranda would call.

"What the hell is the matter with you *now?* She wants you in her bedroom. Up the fucking stairs! How many times have you been here, now? Fifty? Goddamn bimbos." She handed Ariel a fluffy white towel, then stomped off down the hallway.

Ariel fumbled around in the shadows, eventually locating a large circular staircase. She climbed slowly, listening for a voice, music, running water. There was nothing.

"*Ay, chinga.*" A head popped up at the top of the stairs. "*Muy tarde, Mira. Corriando. Rapido.*" A woman in a maid's dress was pushing a cart filled with milk bottles. "*Venga.* Come on."

"Dolores?"

"*Venga, Mira, en la nombre de la policia de Mexico. Rapido.*"

Ariel laughed. Thank god for Nancy Ruiz, she thought.

Dolores took the little gold packet of candy and placed it in her pocket. She pushed Ariel forward, past a huge teak wood door, into Amanda Walters's bedroom.

It was palatial. A bed as large as a boat, carved in rose wood, floor to ceiling mirrors, a Chinese screen with hundreds of geese in flight over a bent bamboo forest, and a dressing table festooned with gold bracelets, pearls, polished ivory combs, and perfumes in fine blown glass bottles.

"*Rapido.*"

Ariel took one quick look around, but before she could breathe, Dolores tugged her into a huge bathroom with a tub that resembled the giant shell in Botticelli's famous painting, *The Birth of Venus.* But it was twice the size and five foot deep, fitted with gold faucets and handles, and rare oils and soaps.

"*Banyo, banyo,*" Dolores yelled, tugging at Ariel's black sheath dress. She began filling the giant shell with bottle after bottle of half and half, till Ariel dipped her big toe into the cool, foamy froth.

"*Fresca, no?*"

"*Fresca, si*, it's fucking cold," said Ariel, sliding into the great seashell up to her face in thick fresh cream. When it reached her belly, it made her shudder.

"MMMMM, mmmmmm, mmmmm," came a voice from the bedroom. "These are the best spearmint leaves in the city. Coming in, dear."

A naked sixty-year-old woman, with silver-blue hair, slithered across the thick pile carpet, and slid into the tub, beside Ariel.

"BBBBRRRRR." Amanda kissed Ariel.

Ariel tried not to blush.

"So naughty to be late, Miss Mira."

Amanda soaked up a huge sponge with foamy lather, and licked Ariel lightly all over her lips, dousing her breasts in milky foam.

It did feel good, the coolness on her skin, down her shoulders in her face, and way, way up inside her where it made her shiver. She felt for a moment like one of the mistresses of Louis XIV.

"You usually giggle," said Amanda. "Are you unhappy?"

"Your girl smirked at me."

"My girl? *Girl?!* This is a *feminist household!* I *never* use that word. Do you mean Dolores?"

"No. The blonde. I'm blanking on the name. She smirks at me."

"Let's soak your hair in the foam to see what color it *really* is. She's Jeanne. She's Belgian. She calls you every week, and you can't recall her name? This is all so nice and cool in the month of May. It's like bathing in vanilla ice cream."

She kissed Ariel first on the neck, then on the shoulders and breasts, tugging her from the tub and dragging her dripping to the shower, where Dolores rinsed both of them off.

"Dry her, Dolores. And watch the carpet, please."

"*Cabrone*," said Dolores, quietly to herself. She dried them both, then covered their bodies with a light powder that smelled of almonds.

"Now leave us. *Afuera.*"

Dolores pressed the packet of spearmint leaves into her mistress's palm and departed.

"Oh, my *Mira, Mira, Mira,* how I want you." Amanda yanked Ariel down onto her bed with pursed lips and intoxicated pupils. "I want you, I want you, I want you."

Ariel said nothing. There were some roles she would rather not play. She held her breath and waited as the purple head moved from one breast to another.

"So you think Jeanne smirks at you, Mira? She's jealous, that's all. Ten years ago, it was her firm breasts I played with right here in this very bed. Now she is too old for me, and her big tits droop down sadly. Not like these."

How nice for you, thought Ariel. *What comes next?*

"That's all it is, Mira dear. Envy. Now I have you. Open." Amanda Walters held out a spearmint leaf.

Ariel opened her mouth.

"You are a joker today, aren't you. I said open." Thrusting her hand between Ariel's legs, Amanda seized at her vulva with the force of a man. "Lay back on the pillow. Open wider. There. Sugar in the sugar spot."

Amanda proceeded to place four spearmint leaves, one at a time, deep up inside Ariel. The sugar crust of the candy scraped against the walls of her constrictor cunni muscle. Ariel began to bleed.

Her blood excited the silver-blue head that bobbed between her legs, searching by tongue until one by one Amanda retrieved each scalloped green leaf, tasting every piece as she moaned and stroked her own little cunt with an electric vibrator.

"You make me so crazy," said Amanda. "I was thinking about your smell all day. And today you smell sweeter than you did last month. Imagine that."

Amanda's tongue made deep thrusts inside Ariel as she extracted and swallowed the last spearmint leaf. All Ariel could think about was cracking the old lady's head between her knees like a walnut.

Amanda Walters rolled over onto her back, spitting out the remnants of green pulp into a silver chafing dish.

How disgusting, Ariel thought, as the silver-blue head began nibbling her clitoris, making sounds like a pig eating slop.

"Does that hurt?"

"Yes! Don't bite it off. It's not plastic."

"Oh, I feel it, I feel it! I wish I could swallow all of you way up into my mouth." Amanda moaned, shaking like a person with cerebral palsy. She grunted and giggled and panted and hissed. "You made me come."

"Good," said Ariel. "Now I have to pee." She got up and moved for the bathroom.

"How was it for you?"

"You don't want to know." Ariel closed the door, then vomited.

She returned, wrapped in a towel.

Amanda Walters, seated at her dressing table, handed Ariel a small silver necklace with three square-cut amethysts, and an embossed cream-colored envelope.

"I'm sorry I made you bleed, dear Mira. I'm not a vampire, but you excite me so. You're to take tea with me today in the salon. I have a guest or two who wish to meet you. Get dressed."

- 3 -

There were six for tea. Amanda Walters and Ariel, in matching paisley dresses. Josh in his black turtleneck, accompanied by Miranda in a red velvet mini-dress. Bonnie Blair all in white. And the queen of talk shows, Rodah Krinkley, who sat on the sofa between Miranda and Josh, looking like a mushroom in a cream-colored suit.

"You see, I found her," said a smiling Ms. Walters to a smiling Josh Perrin. "Just as I said I would. It was quite easy, since Mira Monroe is on my payroll. We won't say for what, now will we, Rodah?"

Rodah Krinkley chuckled "No, we won't. What goes on between two consenting adults--"

Then, dramatically, Amanda rose, presenting the blond Ariel to the brunette Miranda. Despite having been intimate with Miranda for seven months, Amanda never suspected a thing.

Miranda and Ariel rose.

"The cousins O'Brien, together again after how many years?" asked Amanda

"Eighteen," said Ariel. "Eighteen years." She held her breath, carefully scrutinizing Josh and Bonnie. Miranda did the same.

Stu should be here, thought Miranda. *Even he couldn't think up something as crazily complex and Restoration as this. Ariel as me, me as Ariel, and two of our lovers beside us, without a clue as to who's who?*

Miranda squelched a laugh as they hugged. It *was* a moment. There they stood together in Amanda Walters's salon, two actors playing each other. Miranda had it down perfectly. The Tanya pout, the Ariel walk, the Yale affectations, the slightly slutty way Ariel would expose her thighs almost to the panty line and give off that look: *Is anything showing?*

Hugging Ariel, Miranda said, "Ariel O'Brien, my long lost cousin, after all these years. How wonderful. I can't believe it. We're gonna have a lot of catching up to do. We're so different, and yet we're still so alike. We both do the same type of work, generally. I mean, role playing."

"Wow, that was good," Ariel whispered.

Miranda gave her best Ariel pout. They all laughed.

"Actors are *always* acting," Miranda said. "Think of OJ. Who could ever know when an actor is telling the truth, or simply acting? Isn't that true, Ariel?"

The two older women laughed uncomfortably.

Miranda stared at Josh, who studied the two women with complete fascination.

"This is wonderful," he said.

Then Miranda turned to Amanda and said, "I don't think we've ever met."

The blue haired lady smiled. "I know you by reputation. Once I stood across the room from you at the Emmys. You didn't win, but you stood out. That's as close as I ever got to speaking with you, but I am a fan. I think your beauty is without equal. Even by your cousin here. "

Josh was charmed, but the wheels in Bonnie Blair's head were turning.

There was an awkward pause, into which Rodah Kringley plunged. "We should do a show on you two." Rodah was the maven of mush, the queen of mundane, but she could spot the obvious rating prodder as easy as a pimp can sniff out whores. The princess and the slut. "It would have to be a nighttime show, unless Miss Monroe goes mainstream. Gives up porno. That would be boring anyway, and we are not about boring."

"How about Broadway together in a play," said Bonnie. "Broadway does everything these days. Full frontal nudity with carrots up your ass."

Amanda ran her fingers along the edge of Miranda's dress, thinking she was Ariel. "So, Miss Tanya, you'll have to admit, this was quite a surprise, wouldn't you say? How would you describe it?'"

"Coy," said Miranda. "Very coy."

She was more than a little proud of herself. Proud of her cousin, too. They had fooled Josh and Amanda in the most intimate way, and Rodah was completely charmed with everything. But the look in Bonnie Blair's eyes worried Miranda. Bonnie Blair was Broadway, not television. Her stare burned a hole in Miranda's forehead.

"Jeanne, we'll have tea," chirped Amanda.

The dumpy blonde appeared with a silver tea tray, and poured out cups in order of importance, as she had been instructed by her employer. Ariel as Miranda got hers last. Ariel, the blond slut who had stolen her place in Mrs. Walters's bed. Jeanne knew Amanda had been married until her husband committed suicide. Mr. Walters had the real money.

"Of course," said Rodah, seated between Miranda and Josh, "*you two* are the couple every person in the nation would like to invite to tea this week. If I got you both on my show, I could promise a most respectful interview, conducted, I might add, in a relaxed and elegant atmosphere."

So that was the purpose of the afternoon. The great tan mushroom put her arms around their shoulders and drew them down into her perfume. "What would you say to an interview next week? In L.A.?"

Josh scrunched up his nose and looked at Miranda. He'd heard the blab on Ms. Rodah. She turned on those who refused to appear on her show and unleashed everything she'd heard about them to *Flem*, their mortal enemy.

Miranda was thinking it over, looking at Ariel, but before she could get out a word, Ariel said, "Sounds good to me, cuz. From my perspective as an adult film star, any publicity is good publicity, and with Miss Rodah on your side, you simply can't lose. What would you think, Josh?"

The fact that she called him Josh, when he'd only seen her in a porno film, excited him.

Ariel broke through the pause and allowed the Miranda she had become to force events to a conclusion. What was the word? Tautology? She turned to her former best friend and asked, "What would *you* do, Miss Blair?"

Bonnie Blair was still trying to put the pieces together, taking her time, reserving judgment. She was still wondering why Ariel had run away from her at the Beverly Hills Hotel. After a studied pause, Bonnie said, "I've been on the *Rodah* show twice and Rodah has been most kind to me. I trust her. She likes actors. She understands us. Especially women. She knows how to talk to women."

Rodah took her cue. "Thank you, Miss Blair." Wrapping her arms around Miranda and Josh in that warm professional manner she was known for, she said, "There is so much love in the faces of these two young people. America needs to give you both her blessing." Tears came to her eyes. She stood up and dragged them with her across the salon. "Josh and Ariel. Ariel and Josh. America wants you *now!*"

Josh stood up. "Okay, let's do it. Before Air leaves for Malta."

Miranda nodded in agreement, along with Bonnie Blair and Amanda Walters.

Rodah Krinkley became businesslike. She took out her hand organizer and punched in a code. Bells rang, little musical bells. "We'll book you for next Wednesday. The whole show. I'll bump Deaderman."

"The whole show?" Miranda chortled with that Tanya pout. She was beaming. Now they had Bonnie Blair, she thought.

Ariel was amused.

"More tea?" asked Amanda Walters.

"I'd like coffee," said Miranda. They were all having much too much fun.

"Jeanne, bring in coffee."

Josh jumped up. "If you two cousins could please stand next to each other, say, right in front of me, I'll snap off some digitals." Josh pulled out a tiny camera as Ariel and Miranda stood by the window, where the light came in from the tennis courts.

"Here?"

"That's good. I do know one of you intimately, as our most recent photo spread in *Flem* would indicate. But you, Mira, I've only seen on a video screen. And it's so much fun as a devout porno fan to finally meet you in the flesh."

Josh touched Ariel's bare shoulder.

"Same for me," Ariel replied. "I've known you only on TV. I'm gonna send a photo home. To Kodiak Island."

Bonnie caught her breath. Miranda pinched Ariel on the ass as the camera sprayed them with light.

Josh popped off twenty quick shots. "You look more like sisters than cousins, except for the hair."

"Twins," said Bonnie, noting the tattoo on "Ariel's" thigh. "Identical twins."

Jeanne entered with coffee, this time beginning with Ariel and having placed two fresh spearmint leaves on the saucer.

Miranda shook out her hair and laughed, laughing at the blonde she once was, who sat across from her looking just a bit detached.

And so she was. Ariel considered the name of the chess move that matched the moment. Queens Gambit Accepted. That was it.

As Jeanne poured the rest of the coffee, the conversation settled into comfortable chatter. The bartering was over. Ariel had won.

- 4 -

When her guests had left and the tea things were removed, Amanda Walters paused for a moment in the hallway, arranging her thoughts before she pushed open Jeanne's office door.

"Are you happy here?" It was not a question. Rather a dull, flat comment.

"Of course. Why would you ask?"

"Mira told me you smirked at her."

"She's imagining things."

"No, I don't think so. I think you were very snotty to her."

"I wasn't trying to be."

"From now on treat her nicely, or in two weeks' time you'll be gone.

Understood?"

Jeanne held back her rage and said nothing. She was tired of being pushed around by a woman who had once called her "baby." Only last week, Amanda accused her of stealing two pairs of silk stockings, which she in fact did take, but the extras had always been recompense from her grateful employer for services rendered between the sheets. Silk sheets.

Now these tokens of Amanda Walters's affection were passed on to a porno star whose claim to fame was her sexual appetite for men. With sex, nothing is sacred.

"Jeanne," she prodded. "You didn't answer me."

"I'll be nice to her next time."

"Yes, you will. And make sure I'm booked into the Roosevelt Suite at the Plaza on Monday. I'm using the company seats at the opera. A party of seven. My sorority sisters."

"The Group," said Jeanne softly.

"Don't be snotty."

Jeanne turned her head away as Amanda left, closing the door with a bang.

Jeanne was very angry. Viciously so. She fumed for a few minutes, then phoned a friend who knew Bud Jones. Her friend was always asking about AW. Amanda Walters. CEO of Tele-Tech. Was she a lesbian? Jeanne had been loyal to her sexual persuasion and kept her mouth shut, but now that she had almost been given her notice.

Now, loyalties meant nothing.

"Shit, what do I care," she said to herself. "What the hell can she do to me now?"

Jeanne had always worked with rich women, and she knew the one thing they feared was revenge. Timing was everything. She had to play her cards while she was still on the job. Inside, with keys to the cabinets, phone records, and checkbooks. That was the secret. Once you're out the door, you're dead.

She speed dialed a friend.

"Sarah, I need the number of Bud Jones. The guy you know at *Flem*."

"So, she's a lesbian then?"

"You bet."

"Really? How exciting. Bud's had a very good run this week."

Sarah gave her the number.

TEN

On Monday, after driving her boss to LAX, Jeanne called Bud Jones at his home number. "Hi," she said, scanning the notes she had carefully written out in long hand. "I'm a friend of Sarah Reilly."

"Oh, yeah. Jeanne. The Belgian girl. Let me tell you right off, we could care less about Amanda Walters. Our readers don't know who she is and they don't care. She has a zero Q."

"How's your Q for Rodah Krinkley?"

"Rodah Krinkley? That's something different. Everybody knows Rodah. What do you have?"

"First, let's get this straight. I'm not anyone's girl. I'm a woman. I'm a woman who loves women. I've had affairs with a number of famous ladies. Lady you can use, if you can't say woman. Lady is okay. Got that?"

"Okay, Lady Jeanne. You got my interest. Tell me what you know."

"My boss, Amanda Walters, is a crusading feminist and a closet lesbian. She's in the closet because it's bad for business. I know she's a lesbian because I was her lover for years. One of several. Now, I'm not. She threw me away. That's where I'm coming from. Got it?"

"Every word." Bud Jones clicked the record button on his phone. "I still don't know what this has to do with Rodah Krinkley."

"I'm getting to that. Rodah is Amanda's close friend and she likes to watch. She sticks her tongue in every now and then, but mostly she's a peeper. When Ms. Walters and I had sex, Rodah watched. I know. I was there."

"And you have proof?"

"I'm getting to that. No, I don't have proof, but I have the means to get it. With your help. Hello?"

"I'm listening."

"Amanda is in New York this week. She has a little lovely who does porno flicks, and Amanda'll want her back in bed next week. With Rodah. Rodah will gawk while Amanda slavers all over her porno princess. How does that sound?"

"I'm not sure. How does that help me?"

"When Ms. Walters is gone, I run the house. I'll let you and yours in as electricians. You install one of those little cameras somewhere in the track lighting above her bed. I've had parties for my friends here when she was away. She never suspected anything. All the servants trust me. She's easily fooled. Sign in with security, that's all."

"Security?"

"They're outside the house at the gate. They check your truck and write down your name. I wouldn't use your real one, what with the article you did on Ariel O'Brien and Josh..."

"Perrin. Listen, Jeanne. We're on a hot streak here at *Flem* right now, but if you're telling me we can get pictures of Rodah Krinkley in bed with a lady porno star..." Bud Jones took a deep breath and waited.

"That's what I'm telling you, and not only that. She's Ariel O'Brien's cousin. Mira Monroe. They were here together for tea today. You could hardly tell them apart. Hello?"

Bud Jones couldn't help thinking *What if this is a setup?* "Ariel O'Brien has a cousin who's a porno star?"

"Mira Monroe. A blonde. You'll need a truck with a logo on it. Electrician. I'll break a light or two. You send someone to fix it."

"We use Western Electric."

"Good. They'll need to sign in with real ID. They check that at security. You'll need a camera that won't show. I'm sure you know about cameras. The shots you got of Josh and Ariel..."

"We know all about cameras," said Bud Jones. "Everything. "

"Good. I'll get you up there into her bedroom after I smash one or two overhead lights. I'll show you the part of the bed she prefers for threesomes. You set up the camera. Oh, and they tape you when you come in."

"Good to know, Lady Jeanne. And what do *you* get out of this?"

"Twenty thousand dollars. Ten at the door. I want it in cash. The bitch is ready to fire me. How's that?"

"That's a lot of money," said Jones. "When? Say next Wednesday?"

"Wednesday is extra good. The cook is out shopping and Dolores has the day off. I'll give you the address and use *my* phone number. Don't go through security. They'll check you out. Sound like fun?"

"Sounds like what *Flem* calls fun. I'll call you back."

- 2 -

Ariel was on the set of *Professor Max*, finishing her deep massage, when Miranda called. "I'm worried about Bonnie. She wants to have dinner. I think she knows."

"Don't worry, sis," said Ariel. "I'll call her at her hotel. You don't have to see her. It wouldn't work anyway. I don't have time to fill you in on all the things the two of us went through getting set up in Hollywood. She has her kind of fame and I have mine. We're no longer close. I've hardly seen her in the last three years. I'll say I'm too busy getting ready for Malta. Bringing her around was David's idea. He's producing her next play on Broadway. It was a joke to scare Anaca. He likes to play games."

"It would just make it easier if I didn't see her."

"Not to worry. How are your plans for Europe? As Ariel O'Brien? Me? Using my passport?"

"I'm going, aren't I? I get stuck with Anaca and you get..."

"Josh. No, I'm staying away from the whole gang. I *like* your life. Meanwhile, *you* have a chance to be a real TV actress. With your clothes on. While I'm still sore from those goddamn..."

"Spearmint leaves. I'm sorry. They scrape. Amanda is a pig. But she does pay well. Could we get together for an hour or two before I fly out of here?"

"When's that?" Ariel asked.

"I'm leaving Thursday night. For Malta!"

"Right. Sure. How about Wednesday night. Let's take the plane up, and you can fill me in on that little tramp, Mira Monroe. I mean, is her life really worth living? For me?"

"I'll say. Wait till you meet the Coast Guard."

- 3 -

"Okay," said Stu Eister. "Before we finish our little film, I want you to take a look at the real Professor Max. The way he was twenty-five years ago, when he was making his own little film in Super-8. With my wife as his lead. When she was Flavia Finklestein."

"What's Super-8?"

"Before your time, Miss Mira. Little tiny film in a little tiny camera, but what he did changed my life forever. And his too! It'll give you both a chance to dig beneath the skin of the real people you're playing. This stuff is real. Flavia did her first porno for a grade." Stu laughed. "Now look where we all are now. Stupendous is the grandest studio in L.A. When you say the word *studio*, remember, the first three letters of the word are mine. I *am* Mr. Studio in L.A. Our films are everywhere. Transposed to DVD in Mongolia and on the internet. Our biggest markets are China and Japan."

As Stu flicked the remote, Flavia settled into her favorite chair. "Oh, jeez, Stewart, not again."

"Yes, again. God, look at the two of you going at it."

There on the monitor, looking like a forty-year-old Frederick Nietzsche, was the real Professor Max Kovaks. Full moustache and hairy ears, Max the great pre-feminist, fingering Flavia Finklestein's very hairy pudendum.

"He said we were all doing it for art," said Flavia, in a white chiffon dress. "His mantra was *Women did not belong to men. Only to themselves.* Not to their boyfriends and not to their husbands, but to Professor Max, the Moses of American cunt. He wrote out the Ten Commands of Sex for women, and said it came directly from God."

Ariel laughed. "I've heard that line before, only God was Freud. "

"I got him back," said Stu. "We arranged a private screening for his wife. She divorced him immediately. Took the kids, the house, and the car, along with the Spinoza papers he'd stolen from Amsterdam. She had a different view about the Moses of pussy. But Max had part of it right and he gave me an idea. What if we made a film from the woman's viewpoint? Not the normal whack-off flick. Man, look at that!" Stu shook his head. It got him every time. Max had his mouth on Flavia's labia. "And now she screws only women."

Mr. and Mrs. Eister exchanged knowing grins.

Ariel squirmed. "How did you feel about him fingering your girlfriend when you first saw it?"

"I wanted to kill him," said Stu. "Look at the way he had her going there. He didn't even know who I was. Handed it to me for editing because I could cut. But I saw something he didn't. He was just a decadent fuck who liked young girls. I thought 'This film is about how women feel when they get fucked.' That wasn't what Max wanted. He had to be the star. That was the way he wanted me to cut it, but I saw it for what it was. Something real The way women feel. Sex is a reality, right?"

God and Ariel agreed. Sex is real life.

"And that was it," said Flavia. "We quit UC at the end of that semester. Stu hired himself out as an editor in the Tijuana porno trade. Free. As an intern. Just to learn. They were doing almost all the porno distributed in the U.S. at the time. It was a good place to start. Turn it off. They get the idea!"

"Wait, wait," said Stu. "Here comes the best part."

On the tape, Max was mounting Flavia, his round belly drooping down onto her thighs.

"You should write a history," said Ariel. "American Porno 101."

"I should. I learned a lot. I worked there for a year, making almost nothing. But I saw how easy it was to produce. You needed the girls and the equipment. In TJ they used mostly whores. The sound on those films was terrible. Where do you put the mike? You can't stick it right in their faces when they're fucking."

Flavia laughed. "I was dancing at a Gogo Club in San Diego. When we started out on our own, we hired the girls I knew in the club. Stu used what he learned from TJ. We started with soft porn, quality stuff. I was the star."

"That's when she started to dig women," said Stu.

"Porno is really about women," said Flavia, rising and straightening her dress. "In porno, women are in control. We're the stars! Stu got that right. Until women dug what they were doing on film, porno would remain dirty movies for frat kids. Stuff sold under the counter. Small stuff. It had to become art."

"Right. Fine editing, real cinematography, direction, scripts. It all began with Professor Max. Jeez. He has shit on his underwear." Stu Eister pointed to the booth. "Turn it off."

The film blurred to a stop. The lights came up.

Flavia smiled. "Any questions, Mira?"

"Well... You say you *have* Professor Max?"

"That's the next stop on our history tour. We'll show you the real Professor Max as he is today. He belongs to us. He's all ours. We own him. Right baby?"

"Sure do. It's about time you met Professor Max. Right, God is here. Good. God has met the professor. Time for the Metro!"

Ariel took a deep breath and followed Roddick. His eyes showed her the way as she grabbed his hand and he tugged down a long hallway to an actual subway turnstile.

A guard stood at the gate; a five by five iron pumper named Turk who looked like a wrestler. "Everything okay, Mr. Eister?"

"Fine, Turk. Open up."

Beyond the gates was darkness. Turk flicked on the lights. There came a deep electronic whirr and a.whoosh as two bright yellow subway cars zoomed up into the light.

"Who's back at HQ Turk?" asked Stu.

"Just the servants and Ospall. He's working."

The four of them--Flavia, Stu, Ariel, and God--climbed into the subway car. The doors closed. Darkness surrounded them as they sped off up the hill to HQ.

It took four minutes. Ariel tried to smile. She was feeling too much like Ariel, herself. How could they *own* Professor Max?

They arrived directly in front of an elevator.

HQ was a ten-storey building that served as home to Stu and Flavia Eister. Each storey was one huge room with a glass elevator running straight up the center of the building.

Stu was talking to God. "Ospalt's up to thirty. When you were here last, he'd gotten only to Abe. Max is on the ninth floor."

God simply nodded. He had said nothing at all from the beginning. To Ariel, he looked uncomfortable.

"Only up to Abe?" Ariel asked mechanically. She had no idea what Stu Eister was talking about.

"Nine," said Stu. The elevator doors opened and there stood a male nurse in a light blue uniform. "How is he today, Evan?"

"The same, Mr. Eister." Evan pointed to an old man seated in a wheelchair, staring blankly out the window.

"Max! You have oatmeal on your chin. Let him watch cartoons, Evan. Max likes cartoons. Don't you, Max?"

"TOOOONS!" shouted Max, who had once been the foremost scholar in California on Dryden and Spinoza. "TOOOOOONS!"

Ariel approached him. "Can he walk?"

"Not any more. We rearranged his spinal chord." Stu was laughing.

Flavia smiled as she glanced out over the whole length of the valley as though it belonged to her. She took a deep breath.

"Did Max go poop today, Evan?" asked Stu.

"He hardly ever does, Mr. Eister. Isn't that right, Max?"

"TOOOONS!" was all that Max could say. "Want more TOOO-OOONS?"

- 4 -

"So you met Professor Max," said Miranda. "Took the metro to the house. I've never seen him. Stu is obsessed with the man. I hear he keeps him as a pet."

"Catalina." Ariel switched the plane to autopilot, pointing down-ward. "He watches cartoons. Like an idiot."

"Did you see the murals?"

"The what?"

"Ospall's murals? Presidential porno. He's up to Lincoln. Six on each floor." Miranda shook her head and laughed. "They're on the ceiling, so I guess you can't really call them murals."

"No, I didn't. This is all very sick, you know. A man in a diaper who was once a great professor."

"Just money. Too much money, sis. Stu owns a hospital with his brother. They do things no hospital should ever do. So what. Hospitals are a secret society. Someone dies because a dose was tripled and no one ever finds out about it. That's life. Stu gives people leprosy. Now, what do you need from me?" Miranda looked out over the blackness of the sea. "Could we get a drink?"

"I'm in a hurry. This is a short ride away from the Groves and Jones show. Do you have all you need to be Ariel? Let's see. My license, my house, my truck, my keys and Josh. What else do you need?"

"Maybe the card to your medical plan. I might need it in Malta. You have mine."

"Done. I left my bag in your car. Okay. What else? You want my pilot's license?"

"Why would I want that? I can't fly."

"You might need it for the *Rodah Krinkley Show*. While I'm out in Hawaii fucking the Coast Guard."

"I don't think so. I'm gonna keep my cell phone. That's the last link to my old life."

"True." Ariel was thinking. Something was missing. "Okay, sis, let's head back. We both have a lot to do."

"That was a short ride."

"I have to pack for Hawaii. Out there." She pointed out into the darkness, then switched off the autopilot, banking the plane around, radioing her position to the Santa Monica airport. She was in charge. She wanted Miranda to know that.

ELEVEN

Miranda sat with a cream soda and milk, waiting for Josh. It was the drink her stepfather made for her when her mother was in her menopausal depths. On Kodiak Island. His name was Serge. He was Bosnian. He may have been slightly Jewish, but the Orthodoxy he proclaimed was strictly acquired. He dealt in secrets. Electronics and sea charts and mineralogical studies of the Aleutians. He could be easily recognized by those who needed to find him, dressed all in black. Being Jewish on Kodiak Island meant only one thing. The Mormons left them alone.

Miranda had her first sexual encounter at fourteen. Her mother caught her in bed with a boy of her own age and went on a rampage.

"Slut. You're just like your father. I hope you get cancer and die, like him."

It went on for weeks. Serge told her not to worry. "Sex is an expression of love, a quest for love. Don't take your mother too seriously. Have a cream soda and milk."

The taste of the three part cream soda and one part milk soothed her. She had to be witty. She had to be bright. She had to be Ariel.

"He's here. This way." Rodah Krinkley's assistant led the way. "A few legalities before we start the taping. In Ms. Krinkley's office."

There was a firmness in her voice. The word *legalities* was off-putting. *Formalities* was the usual term.

Rodah sat by the window at her desk. Josh was slumped in a leather chair.

"I knew Bonnie first," Josh was saying. "Before Ariel. Ariel was...here she is!"

"Oh, don't get up, Rodah." Miranda sat down gracefully beside Josh. She did not slump. She never slumped, but sat bolt upright, knees together, long legs and silk blue heels tucked under in a ladylike manner.

There was something of the classroom about Rodah Krinkley's office. She was the teacher. Wasn't that the whole thing about her style? She would instruct the masses. Gently turn them to the right path. And when they refused, bend their arms behind them like she did with that director who accused her of hypocrisy when it came to the poor. On the air, he forced her to contribute to his film on the homeless of Atlanta.

The show never aired, but it got into the newspapers. And that was the end of him.

"Okay, you two. There are a few things we need to get straight before the taping begins. First, this is *my* program. I hate the word show. Show means to point out or illustrate, while program, to me at least, means to plan, to guide. That's what I do. I *program*. I plan out what we want to accomplish."

"Okay. Right, Air?"

"Sure." Miranda had it down. She was miles ahead of both of them, just the way Ariel would have been. "We don't live in a democracy."

"No. Not on my show. On my...program it's all about the audiences. Plural. First, the one I pamper sitting out there in front of you, so it seems more live. Then the real one, the one we Q for ratings, the one who buys whatever America sells!"

Miranda felt like she should raise her hand. Instead, she sipped her cream soda. Josh reached for a cigar.

"No smoking. Where was I?"

"Praising your audience." Miranda said it cold, without inflection, but Rodah Krinkley got the point.

"Listen, you two are plenty smart. This is entertainment. I have you here because America wants to watch the sexiest couple in the country. Be coy. Talk about love and sex and money, and all the things they want but will never have. You're young and in love. Don't talk about drugs. Don't give me any inside the business slang, no unsigned deals, and most of all, *don't ever turn the tables on me.*"

"Meaning?" Josh ran the robusto along his nostrils unsmoked.

"Meaning, YOU DON'T TALK ABOUT MY PERSONAL LIFE. *Did I ever want kids? What about marriage? How do I feel about women?* That you'll sign off on. And just in case you think you can squeeze in something sarcastic, a little inside joke for your friends, I have final say on edits. That's why the show is taped. One little uppity cracker tried to get me to say something nasty about JFK. He dared me and then he dared me to say nothing. Be a part of a coverup. Okay, it made me look bad, but *this is my show.* What happened? I killed the whole show. And where is the uppity cracker now? Doing kids books for PBS. You don't mess with Ms. Rodah. But you two know that!"

She held up two serious looking papers. "One for Ariel. One for Josh."

Teacher Krinkley motioned them to her desk. They signed, Miranda having practiced her cousin's signature more than a hundred times.

"And one more thing. No politics. Politics is death on daytime."

Rodah's assistant was waiting at the door. "Let's do makeup," she said.

- 2 -

With makeup on, Josh was having fun with Rodah Krinkley's chief ass-kisser, Marianne Munday. "She keeps you hopping. Keeps you in line."

"Rodah has more money than you'll ever have, Mr. Perrin. Iced tea?"

"Anything stronger? Marianne Munday." Josh was reading her brass nameplate. "Made up name?" *What a beautiful wide body you have*, he was saying with his eyes.

"Iced tea is safe. Makes you peppy, without a diabetic incident." She looked down at her nameplate, then at her breasts. "Marianne Munday is my real name. Everything about me is real."

They were on set, but the set they were on was not facing the theatre. Miranda watched the monitor as the audience filed in. Mostly women under forty. Each was given a Rodah teddy bear, and a Rodah sweater set, and the new Rodah book, *Friends of Friends*. When they were seated, they were served iced tea.

"Well, Josh," said Miranda. "How's Bonnie Blair?"

"Oh, Gajesus, Air. She really wants you."

Marianne Munday brought them both an iced tea. "Ice tea peps them up, but leaves them calm. That's what Rodah says."

"I've seen you at the Firenze Club, off Sunset," said Josh, focusing on Marianne's perfect round bottom, "where they have their own Pep Boys. Bennie, Blow, and Smack."

Miranda got the drift. As Ariel, she was home port for Josh, a safe harbor. *There's a lot going on here*, she thought. *Stay alert.*

"One minute," came a voice from the booth. Miranda watched the monitor.

Rodah was out there talking to her audience, holding up her book.

"Firenze Club," said Marianne. "I *have* been there. Who was I with?"

"I have no idea. I only remember you. That lovely bottom of yours. I live right up the hill from the Firenze Club." Josh tossed her a card with his address and personal phone number.

"I'll call you. Benny, Blow and Smack. That's very funny."

And then they were taping.

Rodah was blowing kisses to a friend in the hospital. "You get well, you lovely doll. We all miss you." An eighty-year-old actress who had been in a film with Clark Gable and just had a stroke.

Miranda caught the blandness of it all. The oatmeal-colored chairs, the sad white jazz without a sax, the soft pale lighting, and the off-gray desk the Queen of Slop would occupy when the turntable turned.

"And now the couple everyone in America is talking about, the lovely stars of *South Coast*, here today with their clothes on. Ariel O'Brien and Josh Perrin. Lovely and lovelier."

There was a whirr of gears and then applause. The audience rose.

Josh and Miranda got to their feet. Miranda blew kisses, as Josh put his arm around her ass. A red sign blinked: **PLEASE BE SEATED.**

The audience sat down. As the camera closed in on Ariel's smile and Josh Perrin's perfect hair, Ms. Rodah landed safely in her favorite pos-turepedic, the bulk of her belly hidden safely behind a bland, off-gray desk.

"Bland is good for billionaires," Rodah once told Marianne Munday, as they enjoyed breakfast in bed in Sils Maria.

"*Josh and Ariel!* Thank you for sharing your love with us, with all America."

Rodah spoke to her iced tea'd audience, and to the nation at large, as though she were president of the fucking country, Miranda thought.

Closeup on Rodah holding up the cover of last week's *Flem*, its biggest seller of all time. A pan to the audience rising in applause.

Where had their iced tea gone? Miranda wondered. The blinking sign popped on again and they all sat down.

Pavlov, she thought. *Orwell*.

"She flies a plane! She shoots! She drives a truck!" Rodah's question was directed to Josh.

Pretty smart, thought Miranda. *All those under-forty asses wedged into velour seats, looking up at Josh Perrin in his tight Italian pants. How is he with his tongue inside your labia? That's what they wanted to know. How long can he keep it hard inside you?*

"She's really...so loving and caring to me," said Josh. "That's what."

Neither woman was listening to him. Miranda knew the script. She had it down. She could play doubles with Josh on her side, and Rodah and Marianne Munday on the other, in this hearts and flowers routine as well as she could suck off Gotthold Roddick in *After the Prom*. She could be Ariel and Tanya and Monica Lewinsky all rolled into one Givenchy.

"What kind of plane do you own?"

"I lease one," said Miranda. "It's easier. Less capital plunked down. No storage fees. A twin engine Beechcraft with..." She could drive back every shot with grace and beauty.

Josh touched her arm. For the camera. For the girls in the front row. He knew she could tear up on cue. That too! America deserved their OJ and Monica Lewinsky and all the rest. But bottom line, she knew it was Rodah's game. Hit a hundred balls at her all at once, and she could drive them all back hitting the corners every time. That's what a pro *is*.

"And you shoot."

"I own a hunting lodge. For women. Every girl should know how to use a gun." There, she got it in. For Ariel. Miranda hated guns. In Alaska everyone owned a Glock or a Colt .45 or a Sturm Ruger, and kept it in the car. For bears, they said. Guns made her feel uneasy. Guns and duct tape and crazy porno fans. Like Josh.

"Uhhh, huh. Well, we'll have to be tolerant here. Chuck Heston is a friend of mine."

Rodah loved everyone. Why not? She was billions ahead and she had just begun. She'd made it on PC charm and calculated warmth and *Toler-ance*. The good Ms. Rodah, the voice of reason.

But behind her almost white smile was an empire of financial calculations and polished plutocrats with A-list socialites all on *her* side, passing on tips on everything from future hit shows, to killings in the art market, with asides on which studios would fail in the next six months, to CEOs who might perish in an air crash before their next birthday.

Things like that. Secret things. Private information. Rodah Krinkley knew how to use that kind of stuff. Advantage Rodah.

On the big stuff, Rodah kept her mouth shut. Insider trading? That was the name of the game she played 24-hours a day, only her trading was people. *Flem* traded names with her. So did the biggest bankers in Hollywood. Not Manny, Moe, and Jack.

"When did Josh first kiss you, Ariel?"

In a threesome, Ariel had told Miranda. *With Bonnie Blair on top.* How about sharing that on network TV?

Miranda smiled for the cameras. "On the set of *South Coast*. Our first episode. It was all very innocent. We were teenagers. It was in the script, but I knew he wasn't acting."

"How did you know?"

"By the way his kiss tasted."

The ladies in the audience ate it up. Ariel and Josh looked luscious. Rodah fixed her gaze on Miranda. "Sooooo, how do you remain a teenager at... What age are you now?" Ms. Rodah served an ace!

Miranda smacked it right back. "Acting. I'm an actor. I could play you if they gave me the role." The audience laughed. "My father always told me cream soda doesn't really taste like cream. You have to add milk or vanilla ice cream, and let it foam over the rim of the glass. That's acting. That's what makes the cream soda taste like cream."

Miranda smoothed a finger over her left breast, prodding the nipple to attention. Not for the audience, they couldn't see. Just for Rodah.

"Acting *is* that foaming cream that comes over the rim of the glass," Miranda continued. "It's the froth on your lips secret to the actor alone. That's the skill that makes it real." She ran her tongue along a line of lipstick, this time for the audience.

Josh laughed. "You got that right."

Marianne Munday giggled in the shadows.

Miranda's shot, right on the line. The words didn't throw Rodah. She was all over what came out of Miranda's mouth.

"Your two TV movies haven't done that well."

Miranda's nipple did throw Rodah off. She'd studied the photos in *Flem*. Closely. Several times. And now the deliberate touching of a private part, that almost purple nipple, queered the moment with sexual tension. Rodah Krinkley blushed, then quickly recovered.

"Ariel O'Brien and Josh Perrin *are* having sex in real life, without the cream soda. Not as actors. The whole cunt-tree has seen the pictures. Or was that acting too?"

"They caught us at it," Josh chimed in, laughing. "Sex is healthy. Between men and women."

That was unexpected. Rodah smirked. *So he has a brain under that perfect hair*, she thought.

Miranda, who loved Orwell, giggled at the triple-speak. *This is like advertising*, she thought.

"Sex between women is good," Miranda said softly. To Rodah.

Rodah gave her a look. Miranda had crossed the taboo line. That would be cut.

Then Miranda spoke to America. "We're glad to be sharing our sex life with the whole cunt-tree, Rodah!"

Josh put his arm around her. "It's healthy." He licked her cheek with his tongue. "Like cream soda."

"Yum," said Rodah. There were sighs from the audience. Iced tea reappeared. This show was safely in the can.

Rodah put her arms around them. Ariel and Josh. America's favorite couple of the week. Josh and Miranda smiled back, each kissing one of

Rodah's cheeks.

When Ms. Rodah loves you, so does America.

Everyone was a winner, even *Flem*, thought Stu Eister.

But not for long!

- 3 -

"I saw it." Ariel was on her cell phone. "That line about the cream soda was excellent. You fooled the whole fucking *cunt-tree*."

"That was my stepdad, the one in Alaska..."

"You got her good. It was almost in code. So much going on there."

"She's really not so tough," said Miranda. "She's all about money."

Miranda had done her job. Her piece of the puzzle was now in place. For whom, she was not certain. Had alarm bells gone off in Dutch Harbor, Alaska?

"Miranda? Are you still there?"

"I'm packing for Malta. How was my acting?"

"You were a great Ariel O'Brien. You fooled Ms. Rodah just fine. Now she's headed my way, Ms. Rodah Krinkley. The blue-haired lady's nasty secretary left a message. She wants me to be the cheese between a slice of Jewish rye, and one of spicy pumpernickel. Monday."

- 4 -

Jeanne worked through the weekend to get things lined up. *Flem* was in place with their camera. Groves and Jones had worked their wireless magic, but they were slow with the money.

Jeanne called several times in a frantic voice. "I did everything you wanted, Ray. I got you by security. You're all set up in her bedroom. For Rodah Krinkley and the blond porno slut. That's top shit. My job's on the line here. She gets home tonight. You said Friday. This is Sunday. Where's my money?"

Jeanne's last call ended with a threat to call the owner of *Flem*, Ruddy Drumrock.

An hour later, Ray Groves called her back. "Meet me at Firenze's.

Know where that is?"

"Hollywood and LaBrea. On a Sunday morning?"

"Right. Out in front. Look for a black Hummer. I have your money. All of it. Don't call Mr. D. That would get us all killed."

"When?"

"Twenty minutes."

Jeanne, who lived in Hollywood, was there in ten. Ray Groves pulled up five minutes late. He motioned her to his vehicle, a new purchase based on the sale of the Ariel and Josh video to Stu Eister.

"This thing is like a tank," said the dumpy blonde.

"Better." Groves gave her a black bowling bag. "It's the whole thing. Count it if you want."

Jeanne opened the bag. The money was in hundreds and fifties. "So what was the problem? *Flem* doesn't keep that kind of cash around?"

"*Flem* pays by check for things like this, but the money didn't come from *Flem*. Bud and I are out on our own on this one. We have someone bigger."

She eyed him, but said nothing.

"You don't want to know," he said, finishing her thought for her. "If I were you, I'd be gone from L.A. by Tuesday."

"I wasn't planning on leaving till she fired me."

"Like I said..."

She nodded. "I have family in Belgium."

Jeanne put the bag in the trunk of her car. She had 600,000 airline miles she'd acquired by monopolizing all of Amanda Walters's travel arrangements with one little agency down the block from her apartment. By five in the afternoon, she had a ticket for Brussels in her fat little hands.

TWELVE

Amanda Walters arrived home late and cranky. She yelled at Dolores for not putting out her robe and slippers. There was no late dinner waiting on the table.

Tang, the cook, was off at his son's graduation. Yale.

"Goddamn fucking servants. I treat them better than anyone else in this fucking city, and what do they do? Betray me." She was yelling at her chauffeur, Tom, who was lugging her bags upstairs. He'd waited patiently at LAX for three hours.

"I'm sorry, Ms. Walters," said Tom. "Tang had this cleared months ago with--"

"With that GODDAMN BITCH OF A SECRETARY, JEANNE. I know. She never told ME." Amanda caught her breath. "I apologize, Tom. The last thing I want to do is yell at you. Would you please order me a meal from Gardens? Something with bay shrimp. And put this very special bottle of wine out on the parlor table. It's for tomorrow."

"Yes, ma'am. Sure is big. Rodah Krinkley called. About tomorrow. She'll be here."

"Good. Thanks, Tom. Ask Dolores to draw me a bath, okay?"

Tom nodded, scooped up the giant bottle of Bordeaux, and carted it downstairs. "How was the opera?" he asked, as he descended.

"Terrible," said Amanda. "All operas written after 1950 stink!"

"I wouldn't know."

That made Amanda laugh.

"Bottle sure is big."

"It's a jeroboam." The word pleased her, the way it rolled around in her mouth.

- 2 -

On Monday afternoon Ariel arrived, hung over and edgy. She parked Miranda's Jag halfway up into a flower bed as Jeanne motioned from the kitchen door.

"You're a half hour late. They're waiting."

"Who cares." Ariel was starting to feel the anxiety of not being herself, of seeing her face everywhere and knowing it was Miranda. All over the country, Josh Perrin's tongue was kissing Miranda's breasts, and even if she and Miranda were the only two people in the world who knew the truth, it bothered Ariel.

"Dolores is waiting. For your bath."

"Fuck Dolores."

Jeanne pushed Ariel up the stairs with a shove, then uncorked the bottle of fine Bordeaux, a gift from Valerie Hottsun, president of Sigma Alpha Phi. Sapph for Sappho. Their little joke. Amanda had re-lettered their college sorority.

The jeroboam of Bordeaux, from Le Conte de Rothchild, was especially for Rodah. She had done the softest of interviews at his estate in France.

"I shouldn't be telling you this," Amanda had said to the sisters of her sorority, at their digs off Central Park, "but Miss Rodah has agreed to watch as I munch on the sweet little tenders of my present attraction. That's what she does. She watches."

They all laughed.

In the old days, Amanda would have shared such a story only with Jeanne, but now there was no trust between them. Amanda's sorority sisters alone got the inside dope, and they all lived in Connecticut.

In the old days, Jeanne would have told Amanda of the needle hole punched through the cork, and the familiar scent of liquid amphetamines. She knew the smell. She'd taken it at rock concerts to stay awake all night.

"Drinks coming up," Jeanne shouted from downstairs.

Ariel had finished her bath. She entered the bedroom in a black silk kimono.

Rodah rose from a chair. "Ahhhha. Here she is. I suppose you saw the program we did with your cousin, Ariel?"

"Sorry. I heard about it. I was finishing up my latest adult extravaganza. Work, work, work." Ariel sat on the bed.

Amanda nuzzled her neck. "Here is a lively wine from the cellars of the Le Conte de Rothchild. It's all for you, my dear."

Ariel and Rodah exchanged glances. Rodah and Amanda laughed.

"It's for you, Miranda," said Amanda. "Mira Monroe. Especially for you. Rodah's had this wine before. Haven't you, Ms. Krinkley?"

"Many times, but not in a bottle *this* big."

Jeanne poured them each a glass. To the rim.

Rodah made the toast. "To watching. Bottoms up."

That's what worried Ariel. Somehow Rodah would end up on the bed with her end up, and she certainly did have a *very* large bottom.

They sipped the wine slowly, savoring a universe of energies.

"*Never* have I tasted such a fine Bordeaux as this," chirped Rodah.

Amanda smacked her lips in ecstasy. "Another glass, Jeanne."

"Complements of Valerie Hottsun," said Jeanne.

Ariel put down her glass. "Who?"

- 3 -

In bed, things began slowly. Amanda wanted music. "Put on the Fauvre. 'La Bonne Chanson,' Jeanne. And you," she pointed to Ariel, "on the bed!"

Ariel settled into the sheets, undoing her kimono.

Groves and Jones were watching it live.

"Only...draw it off," said Amanda. "All off. Leave it beneath you."

Ariel became an odalisque.

Jeanne was bustling around. First she adjusted the music level. Vocal.

"He wrote this for his mistress," Amanda explained, "before she became Debussy's wife. To sing."

That seemed obvious.

"The words are by Verlaine," Amanda added.

"Lovely." Rodah settled into a chair of fine mahogany one foot from the bed. "I don't know French. I took Spanish in school." Her eyes moved slowly from Ariel to Jeanne, then settled on the dumpy blonde. "You know, there's something missing here."

"What's that?" Amanda wondered.

There was a long pause.

"I know we've all been to AA, but...dare I say it? There are private, very private moments that we share when things may happen in a way that... Well, to get where we need to go, sometimes to break down the inhibitions. I always suggest using..."

"What?" Amanda smirked.

"Happy Dust. A little coke, if you have some on the premises."

Amanda smiled. "Jeanne handles all things illegal. Buys them from I don't know where, right Jeanne? I gave up coke when my husband hung himself. Such a fuss over nothing, but AA was a cover."

Ariel laughed. She'd read the story in the local paper. One of those Hollywood scandals where nine tenths of what happened is submerged like an iceberg.

"Jeanne, go get the snowflakes," said Amanda.

"I have to pee." Ariel wrapped the kimono around her as she rose.

Rodah's eyes were all on Jeanne. The unbleached part in her hair, the smeared lipstick, the eyes filled with envy and regret, the darting tongue. She was Rodah's type. Just over the hill, a little belly forming below her navel, the sharp nose dripping from who knows what, the hungry mouth. Rodah could taste the wreck of Jeanne. That over-ripe sweetness heading toward rotten.

Ariel was too young, too perfect for Rodah.

Jeanne brought back an Art Deco mirror and a silver bowl. She poured out a heap of cocaine on the glass, cutting three lines with a razor blade. To each woman present, she handed a two-inch section of straw, checking for the angles of the cameras above.

Rodah eyed her full breasts and hips, the blue-green eyes with too much mascara. So slutty and sallow.

"None for the help?" Rodah asked.

Jeanne eyed Amanda.

"She has a record," said Amanda. "Better not."

They all indulged. Ariel first, missing a trace. Then Amanda, the bent blue head consuming every grain. Lastly, Rodah, who drew off her line with nasal deftness.

Groves and Jones were glued to the monitor as Amanda tugged Ariel back into bed, yanking off her kimono.

Rodah returned to her chair, a foot from the bed. To watch.

"Get the toys, Jeanne," Amanda instructed.

They could all feel it, the roar of chemistry, the coke, the wine, the amphetamines, mixed together in their blood like jet fuel and pure oxygen and lit propane.

Jeanne dumped out on the bed a case of dildos, sensual oils, carved vibrators, and whips. Amanda had Ariel down on the bed, exploring her wet parts with her thumbs.

Ariel tried to hold back the sexual energies that ran with an electric charge through her body. She didn't like sex with women. Two women and a man was an okay arrangement. That could get her excited. But on this Monday afternoon in Amanda's bed, a fury of pleasure burst upon Ariel. She pulled the old lady's head down with a yank, into the depths of her labia.

Jeanne held up a double dildo and Rodah wobbled in her chair. Her juices were flowing. "God, this is *beee-u-ti-full*. Women are such magnificent creatures."

"Then jump in, Ms. Rodah," howled the little blue head who had bobbed up for air.

"I'm here to watch." Rodah was sweating and squirming in her chair.

"Like hell," said Amanda "You want it, don't you?"

Rodah stammered.

"Pull off her dress, Jeanne."

Jeanne approached. Amanda's head bobbed down again between Ariel's thighs.

Rodah rose from the chair, panting and gasping. "All right. Undo the hook in my dress."

Jeanne was careful not to touch skin. She undid the tawny silk dress and pulled it up over Rodah's bulk, leaving a slip, heavy support hose, a bra built for Bruhilda, and a girdle that looked like armor. Piece by piece, Jeanne removed the foundation garments until Rodah stood there in her nakedness, looking more like a country than a woman. Mountains and valleys and forests and rolling hills.

My god, thought Jeanne, *the hairy armpits, the hair on her legs, the sweat pouring down her belly.*

Amanda and Ariel moaned from bed. Amanda was into it. Ariel had lost all control. Had her partner been a hairy ape or a stallion, it would have made no difference.

Amanda grabbed the double dildo, first plunging one end down into Ariel's cleft, then squirming her little pudendum into the other end.

"Oil me up, Jeanne."

Jeanne reached in with a hand full of slime and lathered their instrument until it glistened.

"Hurry," said Ariel. "All the way in."

Rodah and Jeanne stood by and watched as the pace between Ariel and Amanda increased as if they were launching a seesaw into the stratosphere.

Groves and Jones looked on breathlessly. All this was being recorded in that wireless world that connects in a moment to the entire universe.

As Rodah pulled off her last stocking, she hung like a wrestler over Jeanne, who tried to keep from touching Rodah's skin.

"What's that?" Jeanne pointed to a place just above Rodah's urethra where there was a very round scar.

"That's where I had a penis," Rodah laughed. It was the amphetamine talking. She had never spoken of that scar before in her life.

"You were a man?" Jeanne drew back.

"I was a herm. They cut it off when I was a baby." Rodah touched her on the arm. "Now that you've pulled off all *my* clothes, I'd like very much to undress you too."

"I don't... No." Jeanne looked up toward the lighting track, with its three small, hidden cameras.

"For God's sake, Jeanne," came the bobbing head, "don't be a cunt."

Amanda and Ariel were locked in a rhythmic fury, as faster and faster came their breath, faster and faster they moaned in unison, their eyes and bodies and breasts and mouths rocking back and forth as though in a dance of death.

"Oil me up, Jeanne," Amanda shouted.

Ariel was starting to come. Her eyes rolled back and she shook her head. Jeanne reached in and again soaked the double dildo.

"Oil can," Jeanne grinned.

"Oil can, my ass," panted Rodah. "I want you."

"I said *no*."

Rodah grabbed Jeanne's neck and tore off her skirt in one quick jerk. Jeanne pushed back, but was no match for Rodah's muscular biceps. Rodah pushed Jeanne down hard on the bed, her bulk muffling the latter's cries. Jeanne gasped. Rodah tugged at her sweater.

"No," Jeanne cried.

"I could smell that crack of yours halfway across the room," said Rodah. "Such a slutty, slutty, slut."

"She's slept with all my sorority sisters," Amanda gasped. She was trying hard to climax as Ariel fell back in spasms. "Fuck her, Ms. Rodah. Fuck her crazy."

Jeanne was still struggling. Rodah tore off her panties. "Let's see what lies beneath the pink."

"I DON'T..."

"For Christ's sake Jeanne," Amanda panted. "Rodah Krinkley wants to fuck you. Submit. This could make you famous in certain circles."

"I'll say," said Bud Jones, as he and Ray Groves angled the cameras in for their closeups.

Rodah's thumb rammed deep into the seam of Jeanne's pink snatch. Jeanne, who had had no drugs or wine, nothing but water, was whimpering. "That hurts."

"That?" Rodah was sweating and panting like a pig.

Jeanne sobbed. To Groves and Jones, it was a Beethoven symphony!

Ariel struck Amanda's ass with a whip.

The blue head rocked from side to side spraying saliva. "I like it. I like it. I'll come in your face, Mira."

Rodah took the double dildo, still wet with the juices of the other two women, and plunged it deep into the dumpy blonde whose eyes were filled with tears.

"I'm dry and I'm having my period," Jeanne murmured.

Groves and Jones were not quite sure what they were watching, but they had it all, closeups and pan shots, gasps and groans and moans, and the final thrusts of female orgasms.

- 4 -

Five hours later, Jeanne was on a plane headed for Europe. Ariel was throwing up what was left of a bay shrimp salad, head throbbing from sex, heart pounding from cocaine and speed. She felt guilty about the sex. She'd enjoyed it.

On the phone to Miranda, Ariel expressed her concerns. "Something is going on here. There's something big happening. Rodah Krinkley was on the bed squirming like a donkey in heat. With that dumpy blonde."

"She was a participant? Hhhhmmmm. How did you like the sex?"

"I have to admit...it was the first time I ever had an orgasm from a woman."

"She really gets into it. Every sorority sister has been on that bed with me or Jeanne. She gets what she wants."

Ariel was thinking of Groves and Jones. Where were they? Maybe with Bonnie and Josh. "What's your itinerary?"

"We leave for Rome on Friday. Two nights there. Then we fly to Malta in a private plane."

"Cast and crew?"

"The crew's coming by boat. All that equipment. Have you seen Groves and Jones?"

"Nope. I was thinking about them. Maybe they went on vacation?"

- 5 -

Maybe not. The two tabloid reporters were on the phone to Stu Eister.

"We got it all. Everything."

Stu Eister had it right. All he had to do was sit and wait for the perfect moment to let it all out!

THIRTEEN

"Soooooo, how was the flight?" Ariel was having a scotch.

"Okay, till we left the plane," said Miranda. "We were mobbed in Zurich. I had no idea we were so popular over here."

"You have no idea how much money we make over there. I never see a cent of it."

Miranda was relaxing in the bath. "So where are you?"

"Honolulu. Stu's hotel. He owns it. He told me to rest my Volvo."

Miranda laughed. "Yeah, he always says that.

"How do they get away with a name like that? I drive a vulva! Speaking of which, I tore up the Jag. That's why I called. It's in the shop. Not that you need it right now. Something underneath. I hit a rock in fucking Amanda Walters's flower bed. Sorry."

"It's a lease. I need a new one. That is, if I ever get back to being myself."

"That depends on you. How's my truck?"

"Parked at the house. It's in the garage. Unscratched. Why?"

"It's due for servicing. Call Nancy for me. I'll feed you the lines. I can't really call from Honolulu."

"Yeah, okay. I'll do it. Ready for the coast guard?"

"Not really. That double dildo hurt like hell." Ariel sipped on her scotch. "It must be *very* late in Zurich."

"After two. We fly to Rome tomorrow. Do you miss Josh?" Miranda ran more hot water, pushing the fixture with her big toe.

"Of course I do," said Ariel. "He has all my keys. And you?"

"I miss him too. But I miss you more. It feels like you're a world away, sis."

"Halfway anyway. I'd better let you sleep. Night Miranda. Stay safe."

"You too."

- 2 -

"Is this Ray Groves?"

"Yeah. Who's this? How did you get this number?"

"Josh Perrin. The same way you got mine. Money. Listen, I need to see you and your friend, Bud Jones. Immediately."

"What about?"

"Not on the phone."

"No deal. Tell me what it concerns."

"It concerns a taping you did on Monday afternoon without the consent of your employer, *Flem*. Somebody else put up the money."

"Don't know what you're talking about."

"I have the same gardener as Amanda Walters."

"So?"

"Listen, little fuck-face, you guys are messing with some very big players and you're out there all by yourselves. Amanda Walters and her double dildo. You want more on the phone?"

"How the hell..."

"You know the Dublin Club? You followed me there one night when I was with Ariel. Well?"

Groves sat up in his chair, but said nothing.

"How about a forcible rape case. Rodah Krinkley. Some illegal substances..."

There was a click on the line.

"Okay, okay," said Groves. "When and what time?"

"Nine o'clock tonight. Bring your friend, Bud Jones. The Fenns may be there. You could get a story."

"The Fenns are old news."

"Yeah. Better them than you on the front page of the *Times*, right?"

"I'll be there."

"You don't sound very happy about it."

Bonnie Blair laughed from the next room.

- 3 -

"Amanda?"

"Rodah. Aren't you ashamed of yourself, Rodah?"

"I'm worried about that girl of yours, Jeanne. Is she alright? With my weight, I might have crushed the poor little thing."

"She's gone. Left me a filthy note. Gave notice. Told me she's going back to Europe. Belgium. Don't worry. What could she do to you, Rodah? She's a nobody!"

"I should have been a little more discreet. I never take chances like that. This is a huge time for me, with the tabloid thing coming up. I can't let out a whiff of scandal with the FCC all over us."

"They're pals. Pussycats. Your face, my financial expertise, and all the wonders of *Flem* at our disposal. Can't miss. The first tabloid network. All gossip, all the time. I'll give her a fat check when she sends me her address. One thing about poor people, they don't disappear till they get paid. Believe me, she's nothing. She can't hurt you."

"She told me to stop."

"It's my word against hers."

Rodah sighed.

"Listen to me, Ms. Krinkley. You think that little drip is going to take on the world's two leading feminists in a rape case? With *Flem* on our side? It's laughable. She's slept with all my sorority sisters. On their birthdays. They'll all testify against her."

"Guess you're right. Still, I'll send her something nice. To remember me by. I really liked her. I liked her a lot."

"Good. She's gone. Meanwhile, remember my sorority motto. *Keep a stiff upper lip, under your slip.* Stay cool."

Rodah Krinkley laughed her Rodah Krinkley laugh. "You make me feel better."

"We're queens of commerce, my dear. No one can touch us. Kiss,

kiss."

Amanda hung up the phone, returning to a stack of bills Jeanne had neglected to pay.

Rodah was already in makeup. She was weary of the fucking grind. The painted smile, the warm embrace to all her guests, the forced familiarity with her audience. As if any of those animals out there in their living rooms knew anything about her private life.

"Here." She handed the phone to her assistant, Marianne Munday. "You okay?"

"Uhhh, huh. I need a vacation. How's Belgium this time of year?"

"Small," said Marianne Munday. "Small and boring."

Rodah Krinkley laughed.

- 4 -

Miranda loved Rome. It was sizzling hot and the fans were ten times crazier than the ones in Zurich. She'd never been to Europe before. Everywhere she went, people treated her like American royalty. Princess Tanya. She gave them that Tanya pout and they melted. They held up the photos from *Flem*, now spread across Europe. They all wanted to know where Josh was.

On the first night at the hotel, David spoke to the cast. "In Italy they have magazines where guys are photographed having sex with cows. And women. Well, you know that poem by Jeffers, 'The Roan Stallion'?"

Ariel would have known the poem, but Ariel was not there.

"You give them a big smile and say nothing. Nothing. This is the country that invented paparazzi--the *real* thing. Forget about *Flem*. Forget Groves and Jones. Here, they publish *anything*. A famous actress putting on her sanitary napkin. A French diplomat sucking off a chimpanzee."

The entire cast laughed.

"To these people, you say nothing. You give them nothing to photograph. We'll be in Rome two nights. Enjoy it. Go to the clubs, but stay out of trouble."

Anaca James had an idea. "I know a private club. I've been there before. It's way out of town on the sea." She looked to Miranda for help. They'd spent the day together buying shoes

"Good. I like it. How about you, Holly?"

Holly was the one with glasses, the least respected.

"The hotel will give you a limo or two," said David. "You'll be on your own. I'm doing business on the phone tonight. When we get to Malta, everything will be different. Quiet. You'll see."

David left the café, returning to his room.

"Okay, I'm in," said Holly. "But Chaz needs to spend the night with me."

Chaz Tyler was the youngest male member of the cast. The kid. Twenty. "Sure, mom. You can give me a blow job. Ariel, too."

Miranda was trying to recall what Ariel said about Chaz.

"Ariel's been so nice to me on this trip," said Anaca, "I'm thinking, maybe she's not Ariel. More like a twin sister. Right?"

"Right," said Miranda. "I'll give Chaz a blow job if you will." She thought how much like the children they all were.

Anaca was laughing. "Remember the place we did the winter show at? Three years ago. Near St. Moritz? What was it called? The little town that German philosopher stayed at."

Miranda looked on blankly.

"Ohhhhh...yeah," said Holly. It was like spring break to them. "Sils Maria. The Nietzsche Haus."

"Where we all slept together in one bed. Chaz and me and you and Josh..."

Miranda laughed. "I'm still trying to forget that night."

The limos took them all to a club at Santa Marinella, on the seashore. Techno music. Pounding, pounding, pounding stuff. Designer drugs. Chaz wound up sleeping with Miranda and Holly, something Ariel had prearranged without mentioning it at all.

Chaz was very loaded. "Did I get good head?"

Holly laughed. "You don't remember?"

"No. I think I'm bigger than Josh, though. Right, Ariel?"

"I didn't bring my ruler." Miranda decided it was okay to go on spring break with the cast of *South Coast*.

"Josh has a lot more experience, right?"

Miranda was taking her coffee out on the balcony. "Josh is the Albert Einstein of sex, Chaz. That's all you need to know."

- 5 -

Groves and Jones were waiting at the bar of the Dublin Club.

"I'm kind of wondering, Ray."

"Yeah?"

"What would happen if Walters's secretary filed charges for rape?"

"Criminal charges? For Christ's sake, Bud, this is Hollywood. It's about money. Criminal changes are filed for...crime. There are no sex crimes in Hollywood. Sex is a negotiating tool, part of the bargaining process. Lawyers and lawyers and lawyers. Civil stuff. Still, this shit is scaring me. Why choose such a public place?"

"Here they come, Ray."

"On time," said Josh. "Let's sit here. You know Bonnie."

She glared at them. "It's payback time, boys. Look at this."

She flipped Jones a large dark envelope with the imprint FRANKLIN PHOTO LAB. Jones took a peek. A nude, gigantic Rodah Krinkley riding Amanda Walters's secretary. A whale fucking a seal.

Jones took a deep breath. Then handed the photos to Groves.

"Holy shit. Impossible."

Bonnie Blair was smirking. "What you have here boys is illegal entry, illegal recording, rape, use of a banned substance and...for the rest you'll have to ask Ariel O'Brien. Take a good look."

Groves flipped through the pack. Amanda sniffing up a load of coke. Amanda and Mira Monroe fucking. Rodah riding Jeanne.

"Ariel O'Brien's on her way to Rome," said Groves, "with the cast of *South Coast*. I don't see her in this collection."

Josh laughed. "Hollywood has played a trick on you boys. For money. Always for money."

"Is that what this is about?" said Jones. "Money? Is that what you want?"

Josh could see the boys from *Flem* were in a state of panic.

"How the fuck did you get this stuff?" asked Jones, the cool one.

Bonnie stood over him. "Doesn't matter. We wanted you to know we have it. All of it. And don't call Stu."

"Stu? Who's Stu?"

"Stu Eister, fuckhead," said Bonnie.

The bartender, who was told to leave them alone, now approached.

"No drinks," said Josh. "We're not staying. We came to chat with these two gentlemen. We only drink with friends."

Josh headed for the door. Bonnie laughed back at them.

"No Fenn's tonight, Pat?" she asked on their way out.

"Not this early. They show up late. But then, you know that. You were married to one of them."

Josh and Bonnie were out the door before Groves and Jones could move.

"You guys look famished," said Pat, as they passed him. "Not used to the big leagues. Too much fame in too short a time." He gave them a sneer.

The men from *Flem* followed Josh and Bonnie out into the darkness. They watched as Perrin fired up his Maserati and drove off. Groves lit a cigarette. He was holding the envelope.

"What the hell do we do now? They know about Stu. They know everything." Groves held the large gray envelope. "What should we do, Bud?"

"Nothing. We sit back and wait. I'm not sure who has what on who, or who knows what about why, but I'm certain *nobody* wants all this out there in the plain light of day. It's just...the motive doesn't make sense to me. Who could have done this but..."

"Stu. Impossible. Why? It has to be...about money, Bud. What else is there?"

- 6 -

It was about money, but not in the way they thought. The publisher of *Flem* called Groves and Jones in the next morning to face the music.

"Sit," said Drumrock. "Say nothing. Watch. I had two hours of the

Amanda Walters's afternoon cued up on my DVD player." To his right sat two men in gray suits, one with a white tie, the other black. "Our lawyers. Ray Groves and Bud Jones. You don't get to know *their* names."

Drumrock fast-forwarded to where Rodah, Amanda, and Mira Monroe were sniffing coke. "See. Good quality closeups. Three cameras." He shot the disk to Amanda lapping on Ariel's pubic hair.

"Jesus," said the lawyer with the black tie.

"Watch this," said Drumrock.

A gasping Rodah was pumping away on the little secretary, Jeanne. Jeanne was sobbing. "No. Stop."

"Christ," said the other lawyer. "They have that on tape?"

"Digital. I know." Drumrock stood up, shaking his head. "Okay, boys. Explain. This is freelance stuff. You did this on your own. Put in the cameras. Paid off the floozy who works for the dyke."

"They were all dykes," said the lawyer with the white tie.

Groves and Jones just sat there. What was going on?

Drumrock continued. "What I want to know, as your publisher and part owner of this fucking tabloid, is one thing and one thing only. WHO PUT UP THE MONEY FOR THIS SHIT?"

They looked at each other. Groves spoke first. "You don't have to worry about expenses, Mr. Drumrock. We did it out of our own pockets."

"The hell you did. *Flem* has the deal of a lifetime coming up with these two ladies. Amanda Walters and Rodah Krinkley. The two you have fucking coke up their noses, one of them the beloved queen of moral goodness and virtue, forcing a woman to have sex with her."

"You can't really determine that, Rudy," said the lawyer with the white tie.

Drumrock ignored him. He glared down at Groves and Jones.

"This is the kind of thing *Flem* does all the time, but not to our own fucking friends." His face was red as a ripe tomato. "Rodah Krinkley and Amanda Walters are friends of the *Flem* family. In fact, they're part owners. Investors. And..." He paused to catch his breath. "And if you two want to leave this building alive, you'll give me the name of the ENEMY of *Flem* who paid you to do this job."

"Stu Eister," said Groves.

"Who?"

The lawyer in the white tie spoke. "Stupendous productions. Mira Monroe works for him. He's the porn king of the world."

"He's big," said the other lawyer. "Very big. But like you, he's secret about his moves."

- 6 -

When they took off from Honolulu in Stu Eister's jet, Art Hotz was asleep. Moe was studying plans for a new patio at his Santa Barbara home. Donald was playing chess with Angel.

"That one can jump." Donald held up the knight. "See?" He showed her the move.

"Oh, how nice. Is that the only one that can do that?"

"The only one."

The rest of the crew were programming *Professor Max*.

Stu Eister sat alone at a table in the front of the plane, drinking vodka. Ariel was one row back, trying to read a book about World War II.

"You know much about forties music, Mira?" asked Stu.

"What?" Ariel was thinking about Bonnie Blair. Their early years together in Hollywood.

Stu began to sing, badly out of tune. "If you were the only girl in the world, and I was the only boy..."

Ariel laughed her Miranda laugh. "Forties music." She looked up from her book. "I've heard that song, but I don't know who wrote it, who sang it, or when it was written."

"You look sad, Mira. It must be lonely for you. No God. Only you and Inga and Angel. We have to have Inga She does all the ass fucking. And I need Angel to keep me young. There's no one here for you."

"I'm okay, Stu. Moe is here. And there's the crew."

"And we're halfway to Midway. That could be a song. From the Forties." He laughed, then got up. "Why don't you take a look at the Pacific from the cockpit? You like planes, right?"

"They're okay. They get you there faster than boats. I don't like boats. They make me seasick."

Ariel got up, wondering why Stu had said that. Miranda knew nothing about flying. She'd been up with her, how many times? Three or four? And never even looked at the instruments, except when Ariel forced her to.

"Go take a peek." Stu knocked on the cockpit door. "The view is amazing out there. We're almost to Necker."

The copilot opened the door. "You want me, Mr. Eister?"

"Yeah. Give Mira your seat. Let her steer for a while. Go back to the bedroom and take a nap. With Inga."

"Okay."

Ariel sat down beside the pilot.

"I hear you like to fly planes," he said. "See, that's Necker Atole. Just a dot in the ocean."

"Where did you hear that I like to fly planes?"

"Someone told me you have a pilot's license."

FOURTEEN

The thirty-seat Brazilia leased by David Ivy for the duration of the *South Coast* shoot on Malta was an eclectic choice, selected for a specific purpose by the chief himself.

Only David knew why.

He introduced the pilot, Evan Habibi, to the cast. "Evan flew for the French Foreign legion. He's Maltese. He speaks the language. Also English. Also French. Also Italian. Also Arabic."

Evan waved. He was tall and exotic. Not young. "I'm so happy to meet you all. I believe you have a cast member here who flies this plane?"

Miranda thought a moment, then stood up. She'd been doing a little reading. "I fly a Beechcraft B60, but the rate of climb pitch on this aircraft is different. I'd rather land it, than take it up."

Evan gestured her forward. "Sit beside me. I'll give you a quick instruction."

All this David had told Ariel before the trip. "It's publicity," he said. Ariel never told Miranda about it. Nothing about planes.

Miranda watched Evan speak the flight commands in Italian. They were not at Roma Internationale, but at a small airport for private planes and charters, closer to Naples.

"Watch. All engine rate of climb pitch is..." He pointed to the panel. "Much like your Beechcraft B60. So it's a little more complicated Not to worry. The principle is the same. You see?"

The plane rose quickly over the water. Evan added, "We climb to maneuvering altitude, with full takeoff power intact."

Below them was the harbor of Naples and its many ships. A fighter jet shot by on their left.

"Yours," said Evan. "F-16. NATO." Their wheels retracted. "Just as you would do, I'm sure."

"Certainly," Miranda smiled.

"Now we check our crosswinds. Retract the wing flaps. And there you see our course." He pointed to the mapping scope. "Sicilia, then Malta. You say Sicily."

"Yes." Miranda liked him. He was fatherly, not all over her.

"So. Want to take it?"

"Uuuhhhh, no. I'm not cleared for Europe."

"Okay. Questions?"

"Why Arabic?"

"Excuse me?"

"David said you speak Arabic."

"That's not so odd. Maltese is a mixture of Arabic and Italian. It's a bastard tongue. But if you really want to know why I know Arabic, my mother was Libyan."

They were over Sicily. Below them Mount Etna was having a smoke. Miranda felt relaxed. Spoiled, even.

- 2 -

"Hi, Nan?"

"Ariel? How wonderful. I was thinking you were dead."

"No. Just on my way to Malta. I have a little problem with the truck. The undercarriage is banged up. I hit a rock at the beach. The keys are at the house. Could you have my mechanic pick it up and bring it in for repair?"

"Sure. How is it out there?"

"Rome was fab-u-lous. The fans are crazy there. How's Josh?"

Nancy Ruiz hesitated. "Well..."

"Nan, it's okay. I know he's with Bonnie. It's fine. He has his summer, I have mine. That's the way we like it."

Nancy laughed. "That's the way you *say* you like it! I haven't seen Josh. When you're away, he disappears. I loved Mexico, by the way. Thanks for asking."

"Sorry, Nan. I've been looking at my stupid script for the last twenty minutes. Dulls the mind."

"I'll say. Just be careful. Love you."

"You too."

- 3 -

Miranda took a nap for ten minutes in the cabin. She was awakened by David.

"We're almost to Valetta," he said. "The capital."

"I know, I know."

"Evan wants you to watch him land. The walled city of Valetta. Fought off the Arabs, fought off the Turks, fought off the British, fought off the Italians, fought off the Germans. Now they have an invasion of *South Coast*."

"Quick," said the pilot. "It's a real tricky landing."

Miranda looked for the bar that lowered the landing gear. Flying didn't look so hard.

- 4 -

Stu Eister had the whole thing lined up. The plane hovered over a string of outer islands never seen by tourists. They flew past Brooks Banks and Gardener Pinnacles, before circling back over French Frigate Shoals to land at a restricted airstrip.

"God, Stewy," said his newly acquired ingénue. "This is fucking wonderful. I can't believe we're out here."

Ariel was stunned by the beauty of the ocean, the coral reefs, the brilliant sky. She didn't miss *South Coast* at all.

In ten minutes the cast and crew of Stupendous Productions, with all their baggage and equipment, were on their way to staterooms aboard Stu's newly purchased yacht, *Fallopia*. Even Moe and Art Hotz were impressed.

"You two share G." Stu opened the door. "Full bath, Moe."

Moe poked in his head. "Stu, this is fucking perfect."

"Good. I wanted you to see these islands before the techie boys take over. And ruin them. We're in here, Honey Bell." He opened A. Teak and marble.

"Miranda, you're in B. All yours. Good enough for our biggest star?" He opened the door. "Same as mine."

Ariel shook her head. "I'm in here all alone?"

"That's up to you," said Stu. "Wait until you meet our coast guard officers. Compliments of a friend of mine, Vice Admiral Gardener. Pinnacles were named for his grandfather, I think. So?" He looked at Ariel.

"Are you kidding, Stu? This is fabulous." Ariel was speaking for herself, not for Miranda. She entered the cabin and gave back that Tanya pout. "I think I'll take a bath."

"Lunch at one." Stu continued down the corridor, dolling out staterooms. "Ring for service if you want drinks."

An hour later, they were all in the galley sipping vodka, with Stu and an older man dressed in white shorts and a t-shirt.

"This is Vice Admiral Rolf Gardener of the U.S. Coast Guard, a boyhood pal," said Stu.

The older man stood up. "Vice Admiral, retired. Now I'm simply the admiral of vice. Welcome to the outer islands of Hawaii, the wild west end. Before you ask me how the hell we could get away with making porno films of newly graduated coast guard cadets, I'll simply say it's an old tradition. We make them anonymously." He held up a shiny length of black silk. "We use a mask." He put it on. "You don't get to know their names, ladies. Only the real man!"

"Have they been inspected?" Angel asked coyly.

"A full meat inspection," said Gardener. "It's kind of an initiation for them. Like Tailhook, but not in Las Vegas. No tabloids. No press at all. Look around you. What do you see? Just ocean."

They all laughed. It was true. There was nothing but sea.

"My boys will know *you* inside out. You'll know them outside in."

"And they get half the profits from the film," said Stu. "A nice little starting out gift for our officers and gentlemen, don't you think?"

Stu gave the taller man a pat on his shoulder.

- 5 -

Anaca James, ever on guard, was the first cast member to read the script. The cast had settled into three villas on the island of Gozo, the second largest of the Malta chain's five islands. It was four a.m. when the scripts hit the cast members' doors. Only Anaca was awake.

She phoned David twenty minutes later, waking him from a sound sleep. "David, this script is shit."

David wiped his eyes and put on the light. He looked at his watch. "Jeez, Anaca, it's not even five o'clock. Don't you *ever* sleep?"

"I sleep on weekends. Look, I don't know why I came on this fucking shoot. It's all about the little princess. It's all about that fucking wet dream of yours, Tanya. I don't mean Ariel. I don't blame her. I mean this is some girl you knew on a summer trip in, when, 1969?"

"Anaca, I haven't seen the script yet. I'm not a writer. I didn't..."

"Oh fuck, David, don't lie. You sit down with the guys and they listen to your fantasies. They follow you around until you give them what YOU want. Everything comes from you." She was frothing.

"Calm down. Can't this wait till breakfast?"

"No. It can't. We'll *all* be there. With our scripts. Where am I in this fucking story, David? I should have stayed home with Josh. Josh knows your fantasies. He knows when he's not in them."

"Anaca...this is unfair. You have that wonderful scene on the Vespa. Riding around Valetta. It's right out of Roman Holiday."

"I'm with fucking Bruce. Bruce on a Vespa. Bruce is Gregory Peck? Bruce is more creepy than Edgar Allan Poe. Jesus, I feel let down and betrayed. And who's the Italian guy who plays Marcello? Opposite Tanya. Tanya on the boat. Tanya in the airplane. The Italian pilot."

"I'll answer all your questions at breakfast."

- 6 -

Nancy was on her way to Ariel's house to turn over the truck to Triple A when the story first hit AM radio. Hate Radio. It was the voice of Mush Rimbaud.

Cackles, guffaws, animal farts, clicking of teeth, spitting and sputtering and wheezing rolled out of his mouth all at once, as the voice of America's underachievers howled to his listeners what late-night internet followers already knew.

"Thanks to a competitor, who I steal from all the time but never mention--but I'll mention him today--thanks to the Grudge Report to which I be-*grudge*-ingly refer, where you will find, free, *two full hours of profane and immoral and illegal activities!* Perverted sex, illegal drugs, and language that is not to be believed, coming out of the mouth of the sainted *liberal* Rodah Krinkley."

That was the way it began as the sun came up on Malta.

"According to my spies--I haven't watched the performance myself, he said on the advice of counsel--Ms. Krinkley was engaged in *lesbian* sex in the same bed as the star of adult entertainment, Mira Monroe, though Krinkley was not engaged in sex with the porno superstar. No.

"All this at the home of electronics mogul Amanda Walters, major contributor to Democratic women's causes. Are you shocked? There is even a possible rape on the two hour, triple X showcase of liberal immorality. But the woman involved, according to Grudge, has fled the country in fear of her life.

"We've called the LAPD on this matter. The same West L.A. office that handled the OJ murder case. They refuse to comment, saying only that no charges have been filed. They have just begun their investigation of Rodah Krinkley and Mira Monroe, ladies and gentlemen.

"How do you like that? And except for Mira Monroe, I've been told, they're not very pretty."

- 7 -

That was the unkindest cut of all.

Rodah Krinkley got the first call from her lawyer. He was boiling.

"This whole thing is like a runaway freight train," he yelled. "The fucking internet. No wonder the Chinese Communist Party monitors *every* fucking computer hooked up in China."

"What do I do?"

"You do nothing. You don't say anything."

"But I'm on the air."

"You say you're sick. You need an operation. You put on reruns."

Rodah next heard from her negotiators with *Flem*. They were respectful.

"The thing is, you need to lie low, Ms. Rodah. That's what our PR people tell us. The deal can still go through, but not right now. The FCC would eat us alive."

"I have serious money tied up in this."

"We do too."

They were nameless, faceless people at the end of the phone line. To Marianne Munday, Rodah complained face to face. "Someone set us up. Who would you suspect?"

"See how long it takes for Amanda Walters to call, though it couldn't be her."

"It couldn't. She'll lose almost as much as I will. And did you see her on the monitor? That little head of hers bobbing up and down. One of the girls must have done it."

"Don't use that word."

"One of the younger women."

Amanda was at a spa in Ojai, taking a mud bath, when she heard the story on the radio. She called Rodah immediately.

"Rodah, have you seen it?"

"All two hours of it. Where are you?"

"Shaherazade Beauty Ranch. I heard that fat fraud on the radio. Imagine him calling me a Democrat. I'm a lifetime Republican. Have you spoken to your lawyers?"

"Several. They tell me to lie low. Do nothing. Go off the air for three months. Take a trip to Raratonga."

"Where? I mean, isn't there anything we can do, legally? "

"That's not the point. It's on the internet. Everywhere. My fat ass and your pink little tongue. For all the world to see. You can't stop it. You can't shut it down. In the old days, when Otis Chandler ran over an old lady and killed her, the story disappeared from all media by 7:30 a.m. This is the internet. It's probably in Mongolia by now. Mongols are giggling in their yurts, with you lapping off that blonde's little clit, and me plunging a double dildo into your secretary."

"Ex-secretary. She's gone. No, lawyers can't help us. The media can't help us. When my husband hung himself, there wasn't a sound in the media. Nothing. Those days are gone. We're living in the age of internet terror! How does my hair look on screen?"

"You look great, Amanda. Trim and perfectly coiffed. I'm the one who looks like an out of control baboon. The closeups are incredible. Mouth to mouth. End to end. In your bedroom. They panned all over your paintings and jewelry. All out there on display. It's like a home invasion robbery. Whom do you suspect?"

"They had very sophisticated equipment. I'll check with my security people. Jeanne let them in, but I can't figure who would be behind it. Someone who hates us both!"

"That's for sure," said Rodah. "Someone who wants us dead."

- 8 -

Before the story hit the evening news with the force of a nine point earthquake, Josh had the two hour sexcapade in Amanda Walters's bedroom burned on a DVD. He was showing it on his giant TV to a delighted Bonnie Blair.

They watched from the couch as the little blue head of the electronics mogul bobbed up and down, over the body of her blond porno star, counterpointed with the grunts and thrusts of the rotund Rodah Krinkley, thrusting her rusty double dildo into the squeaky labia of Amanda's secretary as she screamed in pain.

"Well, Broadway Bonnie?" asked Josh.

"This will finish them all, the rich fuckers. There's nothing worse than being the butt of everyone's jokes, from Leno to Rimbaud. They're dead in the water, gone forever. Turn up the sound, Josh."

He did.

"Suck it all down," gasped the older woman.

The dumpy blonde was sobbing. "Get off me, you tub of shit."

Josh shook with laughter. "This will sell more copies than the Bible. God, Mira looks so much like Ariel. Watch for the striations on the minor labia. Exactly the same."

"I met her when I was ten."

"Mira Monroe?"

"Miranda O'Brien. At summer camp. In Alaska."

"Come on, Bonnie. How come she didn't know your name?"

"It wasn't Blair then."

"Gajesus. Look at that woman's asshole."

They laughed uncontrollably as the lens focused on Rodah Krinkley's anus.

- 9 -

"Ariel?"

Miranda recognized the voice. "I'm sound asleep, Nan."

"I had to call. It's all over everywhere. There's a thing on the internet of some old lady and your cousin. The porno star, Mira Monroe. Rodah Krinkley's in it too. All in bed together. Everyone's talking about it. It just broke on the local news. I thought you should know, since you and Josh were on her show. *Rodah*, I mean. "

Miranda shook herself awake. "Does the old lady have blue hair?"

"Yeah. She does. How did you know?"

"I guess I should call..." She stopped to think before speaking the name. "Josh."

"Why him? He wasn't in bed with them."

Miranda held her breath. "Look, I'm really tired. Let me get back to sleep." She hung up the phone, but wondered about Ariel out there on French Frigate Shoals.

On Stu Eister's Yacht. Away from everything.

Somewhere, Miranda had notes on how to reach them ship-to-shore, but decided to let it go. Ariel had become her. She liked being Miranda. Ariel was the one in the video with that blue head bobbing up over her nipples.

Miranda was Ariel. She was Tanya. She was on the cover of *Flem* with Josh. She thought for a moment, but decided to do nothing at all.

She fell back asleep and let the whole thing go.

FIFTEEN

It was an old dream. She dreamed it every time she was away from home. Away from the safety of her own properties. She and Miranda were on the beach at Mystic, Connecticut. A hot day in summer. They ate cut peaches together on a red plaid blanket, in their little girl's bathing suits, with the chop of the Long Island Sound playing soft water music in the distance. Peach juice ran down their chins as they rushed to the surf, flinging a red rubber raft out onto the almost waveless water.

It was always the same.

The faces of their parents, strained, not smiling, waving tensely as the two girls floated up on the waters together, paddling out into the deep until the faces on the shore faded, and Ariel and Miranda balanced together on the little red raft. Two lost waifs on a lettuce-green sea.

Then the winds came up. They struggled together, holding on, crying, until Ariel felt lost in the murky waters. The sky darkened. Ariel struggled to keep afloat. Miranda sank into darkness.

It always ended with Ariel gasping for air, struggling in huge waves, then sinking down.

She awoke smelling breakfast meats cooking in the galley. Stu and Angel were laughing together in the adjoining stateroom.

Ariel opened her eyes. She looked at her watch. Seven o'clock. It was daylight. Outside her porthole, the sea was a bright, shiny aquamarine, vast and unrumpled by wind, dazzling with the early morning sun.

- 2 -

Fans crowded the streets of Valetta. The Maltese police held them back. David was not pleased. "We'll have to loop in the sound." He was talking to Larry, as Bruce and Anaca passed the crowd on the Vespa.

Bruce waved. The crowd cheered.

"Maybe we can use that," David said. "Save it for the promos."

Miranda liked to watch them do exterior shots. She was off for the morning. No makeup, no nothing. She sat at a café table that was part of the set. For a later scene. She had her lines down.

The Italian actor, Dino, sat down beside her. "You see this part? We fly out over the coast near a Roman ruin."

"Ummm, hmmmm." Miranda was repulsed by him. The standard Italian type, in tight black pants, smoking Galois.

"Where do you think that would be?"

"I have no idea, Dino. David always has these stunts. He likes to be in one scene a year, like Alfred Hitchcock."

"*Psycho*. Oh, yes. Was he in that?"

"I don't think so."

"It's all very funny, with me playing a pilot and you *being* one."

"Who told you that?"

"David. Did he tell you about the plane?"

"No."

"It's the same one we flew from Naples. Embraer 120 Brasilia. Thirty passenger."

"That section's missing in the script."

"Maybe David has a surprise for us. Maybe he has a secret."

Miranda didn't like surprises and she didn't like secrets. "What's this part about Roman ruins?"

"You've flown a plane like that before? A two engine, propeller driven--"

"Dino, for godsake, please. Let me prepare."

He laughed. "Let you prepare? That sounds like a brush-off line "

It was.

- 3 -

Bonnie Blair lay on the bed, her legs spread. Josh had his digital, high-power, quick focus camera going.

"Look up on the monitor," he said.

"I'd rather not. How's your movie role?"

"Got it locked up. Drumrock Productions. You smell like licorice."

"Anisette. Don't you ever get tired of poking around inside a girl's sexual organs?"

"Only if they're fat and ugly. So you know about David's stunt?"

"I've heard something," Bonnie smiled. "I know everything, Josh. That's why I'm the reserve lover. On the bench for Tanya."

"You think it's safe?" Josh looked her in the eyes. "There's always a risk. Maybe David should tell her?"

"If he did, that would make it criminal. Ariel's a big girl. Right?"

"Right. How's your play going, Blair?"

"We start out in Hartford. All ladies."

"How sad for you."

"Yeah."

- 4 -

In the afternoon, the cast and crew of *South Coast* took off from Valetta with exterior cameras in place.

"We're heading south," said David. "Toward Africa."

The cast luxuriated in the front half of the plane. The crew cramped themselves in the back, huddled over their equipment.

The pilot broke in. "We'll be flying at ten thousand feet, low altitude. Cruising speed 340 mph. The day is sunny, very hot over Libya. 110 degrees."

David handed out the missing pages of the script. A cameraman was in the aisle, testing the lighting.

Bruce looked worried. He stood up as he accepted his pages. "Libya? Who said anything about Libya?"

"It's the scene where you are all fighting in the aisles. Throwing food at the flight attendant. Check your sides. It says we're flying over Leptis Magna, the largest Roman city in north Africa." David pushed Bruce back into his seat. "This has to be perfect."

"Libya?" said Anaca. "That's Khadaffyland."

"Right, but our pilot is half Libyan. He holds dual citizenship. He got permission. We fly very low over this amazing city, almost intact. It's like..."

"They turned the water off two thousand years ago," said Anaca. "I read it in the guide book. Malta and north Africa." She held up the blue book.

"Thanks. So, let's look at insert 1A. The food fight. It's supposed to be light. Holly is mad at Bruce. Ariel is sore because the pilot is not taking the time to point out a flotilla of sailboats. Stock shots. Ariel suspects he is involved with our Maltese flight attendant. Stand up, Gabriela. It's a funny scene. Bruce throws his salad at Anaca. Anaca splashes her drink on Gabriela. Then Ariel rushes up the aisle and says *I'm going up front.* See that?"

"Yeah."

"That's where I jump in," said David. "My moment of glory. A passenger on *South Coast Airlines*. Gabriela tries to restrain you, Tanya. You fall on my lap, and I have my one line."

"Okay, look down," said the pilot.

They were over the Mediterranean Sea, approaching a ruin as large as Cleveland.

"Gajesus," said Miranda, "look at those streets."

They all looked down.

"Okay. Got that on the monitors?"

"Exteriors have it down."

"Let's make one pass. I want you all ready for the scene. If we're lucky, we can do it in one take."

"Camera A, ready to role?"

"Got it set."

"Okay. Let's have lights."

"Now, Anaca?"

Anaca squirmed in her seat. "You're sitting on my new mantilla."

Bruce got to his feet. "Sorry." He spilled his drink on purpose all over her summer dress.

"You soaked me, stupid!"

The whole cast laughed.

"I'm all wet. Flight attendant, could you help me out here?"

As Tanya rose, Gabriela pushed her down into her seat. Hard. "You'll have to stay seated, miss."

"Okay, the plane rocks here," said David.

The pilot tilted the right wing upward as they made a low pass over the forum of the ancient city.

"Your eyes show fear, Anaca."

The plane wobbled. The entire cast were in harmony here. They all showed fear. No acting involved.

Anaca's salad slid from her tray table onto Bruce's lap. Bruce grabbed the salad plate and threw at Gabriela. Tanya gave him a wry smile.

"Good," said David. "Got it. Let's head back. Ariel, I want you in the cockpit for your scene with Dino."

They looked out as the plane rose again. There were no fighter planes from the Libyan Air Force approaching, but the hearts of the actors were still racing.

It was thirty miles out of Valetta where the whole thing started to come apart. Miranda was finishing her shots with Dino in the cockpit.

"Out there is Sicily," said Dino.

Just a look from Tanya.

"If you look real hard on a clear day, you can see the smoke from mount Etna."

"I see it," said Miranda.

They had finished the scene. They were on autopilot. The real pilot was having a smoke with the crew in the back of the plane. Smoking is permitted in Malta. Things are relaxed in Malta.

"Piettro, time to fly us home." David walked to the rear of the plane and handed him a drink. David looked tense.

"Shouldn't be more than ten minutes," said the pilot.

"Yeah, easy." David headed for the men's room. "Good day's work. Keep the cameras rolling."

Halfway up the aisle, Piettro started to choke, then fell over Bruce. Piettro gasped and turned red. Dino and Miranda were still in the cockpit.

"Get this jerk off me," yelled Bruce.

"His face is purple," yelled Holly.

David rushed into the cabin. "The pilot has had an occurrence."

To Miranda that sounded almost like a legal term.

"Did you hear what I said? You'll have to fly the plane, Ariel."

"Me?"

"You have a license to fly on instruments. Two engine planes. That's what this is."

Miranda cleared her throat. "I don't speak Maltese."

"English is the primary language on Malta. It's the only English speaking European..."

"I speak Maltese," said Dino.

"Then get on the radio and call in our position." Somehow, to Miranda, David seemed cool and well organized.

Dino put on the headset. He checked the course line, the turn coordinator, the heading indicator, the altimeter. To Miranda, he seemed to know what he was doing.

"Valetta Tower, this is flight MXT25. We have a pilot down."

"Valetta tower. What are your coordinates?"

"We're at..." Dino turned to Miranda. "Where are we?"

Miranda was unable to speak or think. She could hardly breathe.

"Valetta Tower to Flight MXT25. You have a licensed co-pilot on board?"

"No. We have an American pilot who is licensed to fly this aircraft," said Dino.

"Name?"

Miranda could hardly say it. "Ariel O'Brien."

"The actress?"

"*Si*," said Dino.

"You're fifty miles out. Take it down to five thousand feet for approach."

Dino eyed Miranda. "Extend flaps." He pointed to the controls.

"Pull."

Miranda made a weak effort.

"Harder."

She pushed at the controls, extending the flaps with a quick jolt. It was like hitting a wall. The cabin veered left, then right.

"Extend landing gear."

Miranda looked down the end of Dino's index finger to a lit-up red button. She pressed it and heard the whirring sound of a motor, then the thud of metal wheels as the landing gear snapped into place. That much she remembered.

"That's good, Ariel. Flight MXT25 to Tower. Landing gear in place. We're at 420 kph with an altitude of 3420 kilometers."

"Maintain an angle of ten degrees descent."

"Come on, come on. This is important." Dino watched for Miranda's hand to move, but it did nothing.

"Flight MXT25?"

Dino looked at Miranda. She was frozen to her seat.

"Flight MXT25 cleared for emergency approach. Descent at ten degrees."

"Ariel, for godsake, I can't do the rest."

"I'm not Ariel."

"What the fuck are you talking about?"

"I'm not--"

"Flight MXT25, cleared for emergency landing."

"I know this is a setup, and you're a--"

"Flight MXT25, your rate of descent is too steep. Abort landing. Pull up your flaps."

Miranda reached for the lever, but pushed it backwards. The flight speed dropped--from 340 kph to 220. Dino grabbed the lever and shot up the speed to 300 kph.

The cameraman was scrambling down the aisle, when the plane went into a clockwise role, overshooting the airport, rising for a minute or two, then falling in a dead stall to crash on an island occupied only by farmers and goats.

The Brasilia burst into fire upon impact. The entire load of passengers was consumed in flames almost immediately, burned beyond recognition.

- 5 -

The news reached Ariel indirectly. Stu Eister was in his stateroom listening to a satellite radio. Cool jazz. Ariel lay sunning herself in a deck chair, almost asleep. Halfway through John Coltraine's *Lush Life* the station announcer broke in:

"It's a sad day for the fans of *South Coast*, that show with the perennial teenage heartthrobs. While filming an airline scene off the coast of Africa, their plane crashed, killing every passenger on board. It's believed the entire cast has perished, except for Josh Perrin, who's off making a film in Santa Barbara. Also on board were the show's director, David Ivy, Italian actors Dino Maretti and Gabriela Tasso, and most of the regular crew of the show. *South Coast's* distributor, Avatar, mourned the loss of their famous cast, with the statement 'They will live forever'."

"Holy Jesus," yelled Stu. "How the fuck could that happen?"

Ariel thought for a moment, then wondered about calling Nancy Ruiz.

She had to think it through.

SIXTEEN

"Stu?" asked Ariel, on deck. She had been reading *Being and Time*.

"Huh?" Stu Eister was prodding his Palm Pilot with a nervous finger.

"Ariel O'Brien was my cousin."

"I heard that. Yeah. So?"

"Well, there's supposed to be a memorial in three days. For the whole cast of *South Coast*."

"Except Josh Perrin. So?"

"So, I want to be there. I have to be there."

"Mira, we're in the middle of the fucking Pacific, shooting our biggest budget film of the year. We have the coast guard standing by. Even if you could get out of here in a day or so, do you think I'd let you go? Stupendous Productions has big money tied up in this shoot. You're the star. How the hell did you think we could convince a vice admiral to produce the military dick here? I mean, you know me. I'm a nice guy. But don't push me too far or..."

"Or I might end up like Professor Max, right?"

"Right. I mean, what are you gonna do? Hop on a jet, Mira? For godsake, let it go. From what Bonnie tells me, you were never that close. Since you were kids."

"Bonnie?"

"Bonnie Blair. She knew you both."

If Ariel had been Miranda, there never would have been a thought of leaving. Miranda followed orders. The boys who make the noise were all over her like clam shit. They owned her. They petted her head like a poodle. But not Ariel O'Brien. Ariel O'Brien did her own thinking.

Forty hours later, Ariel was back in Los Angeles, talking to Nancy Ruiz. "Nan, don't hang up. This is Ariel."

"What kind of a sick joke are you trying to play? Ariel's dead."

"Look, click off your cell, then speed dial my number. How would I get your cell?"

"Come on. The cast of *South Coast* all went down."

"That was Miranda. Miranda, my cousin. Mira Monroe. Not me. I don't know what happened out there, Nan, but all I do know..." The phone clicked dead.

Two minutes later Ariel's cell phone rang.

"That's why you sent me on vacation?"

"Right."

"I'm still not convinced."

"My ranch goes to Josh and my house goes to you. How's that for proof?"

"Who knows?"

"No one. Well, I'm not entirely certain of that now."

"You mean, Josh might know?"

"He might."

"Where are you?"

"In a car headed towards Malibu. I need your help. I can't go to my place. I'm a ghost. You're my executor, as you already know. You have the right to enter the premises."

"Okay. Tell me what you need."

- 2 -

The funeral for Ariel O'Brien and the entire cast was held at Wooded Meadows on the first day of June. Ariel came as Mira Monroe, a blonde. She stood quietly in the background, watching as her parents mourned her death. For a moment they eyed her, cousin Miranda, but were told by Nancy Ruiz, Ariel's dedicated employee and executor of her will, that Miranda was a porno star.

Josh noticed her too, but chose to do his mourning with Bonnie Blair.

Ariel wept quietly as the Episcopal minister spoke for the families of all the cast when he said, "What great sadness we feel today when such a fine young collection of delightful energies has been taken from us, taken from the entire world in such a way as to leave us with nothing to say at all. For this great tragedy, only tears and sorrow will suffice."

There was great weeping. The TV cameras caught it all, missing only Ariel herself, who stood outside the ring of grieving families, friends, and fans. Only Bonnie made any effort to speak with her.

"Miranda?" Bonnie was cold as ice.

"You knew us both." Ariel shrugged her off.

"I'm really sorry."

"Just fuck off, will you?"

The next day the front page of *Pro Dough* read: SOUTH COAST IS NO MORE.

Three days later, Amanda Walters and Rodah Krinkley were arrested. Groves and Jones had turned state's evidence. Jeanne, the dumpy blonde, was on her way back from Belgium. There was a search out for Miranda O'Brien.

But Miranda O'Brien was gone. Off the radar screen. High in the air in a two engine Beechwood B60, headed for a quiet place in the South Pacific, west of Raratonga.

She made one call before she left. To Stu Eister. He was still in Hawaii.

"The cops know all about Professor Max, Stu. In case you want to find me."

"The cops have known all along. They don't care. And why would I want to come after you, Ariel? You allowed me to do what I do best. Bring pleasure to the little people, and disaster to the boys with the biggest toys. I got them all."

"You knew about Miranda?"

"Bonnie knew. She knew everything. All the pieces. Josh told her about the stunt David had in mind. She figured out the rest. I've picked up her new show. A month in New Haven, then on to Broadway.

Bought it from Drumrock. He's on his way to meltdown hell. Come see us when you're in New York."

Then he clicked off.

End

CPSIA information can be obtained at www.ICGtesting.com
Printed in the USA
BVOW07s2303230215

389021BV00001B/22/P